Illegal

Miriam Halahmy

Titles in this series in reading order:

Hidden
Illegal
Stuffed

meadowside
fiction

First published in 2012 by Meadowside Children's Books
185 Fleet Street, London, EC4A 2HS
www.meadowsidebooks.com

Text © Miriam Halahmy
Brickwork element of cover image (Derelict 1) © Chris West
www.chris-west.co.uk

The right of Miriam Halahmy to be identified as the author
of this work has been asserted by her in accordance with
the Copyright, Designs and Patents Act, 1988

A CIP catalogue record for this book
is available from the British Library
2 4 6 8 10 9 7 5 3 1

Printed and bound in by CPI Group (UK) Ltd, Croydon, CR0 4YY

Illegal

Miriam Halahmy

meadowside *fiction*

For
Elliott and Ruth
with love

"There is something rotten in the state of Denmark."

Hamlet 1.2 by William Shakespeare

And if you come, when all the flowers are dying
And I am dead, as dead I well may be
You'll come and find the place where I am lying
And kneel and say an Ave there for me.

from 'Danny Boy', lyrics by Fred Weatherly

Chapter 1
Empty

Lindy opened her eyes and stared at the cot. Swinging her legs sideways, she sat up and leaned over the wooden bars to straighten the pink flannel sheet as she did several times a day. Sean had laid out his cars at one end in a neat line. She looked at Sean in his bed by the door. His thin face peeked out from the duvet, eyes closed, mouth open. There was a slight whistling sound as he breathed in and out.

Have to get it now, before he wakes up...

Sean's inhaler lay abandoned on the floor next to the clothes he had tugged off the night before. Crossing the room on bare feet, Lindy bent down, eyes still on her sleeping brother and picked up the small, grey object. She shook it. Was it full or empty? There was a slight rattling sound.

It'll have to do.

Sleepily, Sean opened his eyes. Lindy froze, half bent, pushing the inhaler behind her palm with her fingers.

"What's the time?" he mumbled.

"Eight. I've got the bathroom first," and grabbing her clothes she went out into the corridor.

She passed her brothers' bedroom. The door stood open revealing a jumble of bedding and clothes. Garth's mobile

9

phone lay on the floor next to the bin. She'd tried using it once or twice but the credit had run out.

Her two older brothers were 'away', as her Dad liked to say. He never said Young Offenders' Institution. Neither did her brothers, although they were in and out often enough. They just said 'prison'. But this time Garth was nineteen, so it was even more like proper prison. The thought made her shudder.

If only Garth was here, he could have done something, got me out of this mess.

She was in so much trouble and she had been too stupid to see it coming. If only she'd stopped to think, not jumped in feet first, she would have realised and then she'd never have got involved. She should have checked with Garth first, sent him a letter or begged the neighbours to use their phone to call him in prison. Her family never paid bills so the phone had been cut off for months.

But I didn't and now it's too late.

She could hear Mum and Dad snoring as she passed their door. No chance they'd wake up. They didn't get up before midday.

Lindy went into the bathroom and closed the door behind her. She wedged a towel along the bottom. The lock had never worked and she had to stop Sean barging in.

She washed and dressed and then, taking the inhaler, shook it the way she saw Sean doing each morning. "My puffer", he called it. Staring at herself in the mirror, pale skin dotted with freckles, curly red hair loose around her face, she put the puffer in her mouth. She pretended to press the button and took a deep, rasping breath.

Was it convincing? She wasn't sure, but it would have to do. She'd thought about skipping school but she'd already been in trouble for that. They'd sent the officers round. She couldn't risk that again.

They ask so many questions. What if they find out what I'm really doing?

She couldn't undress for P.E. Not today, not this week. Probably not for a couple of weeks. She had to make the teacher believe she couldn't run about today.

At least it was English first thing. They were doing *Hamlet.*

Mr Davies, the English teacher, had told them, "Hamlet's uncle killed his father and married his mother. He had no one left to turn to. Hamlet was a spiritual refugee."

A spiritual refugee. Lindy liked that. *Just like me. I've got no one left at home either.*

Lindy had underlined Hamlet's words, 'Then it started like a guilty thing, upon a fearful summons.' Mr Davies had yelled at her for marking the book but she didn't care. When he wasn't looking she had torn the page out and tucked it in her shoe. She knew all about guilt, didn't she?

Checking her reflection in the mirror once more, she kicked back the towel from the door and went out.

Chapter 2
Exposed

"Since when do you have asthma?" said Jess, posing in front of the cracked mirror in her bra and thong, her long bare legs tanned a golden brown.

The other girls were changing into shorts and T-shirts and they all turned to stare at Lindy. She felt herself go hot in the crowded changing room. Her hand closed around Sean's puffer. No one would stand up for her, she didn't have any friends. For the past two years she had always been rushing home to be with baby Jemma.

Jess smoothed salve over her bottom lip and, still staring in the mirror, called out, "Lindy Bellows with asthma. Didn't even know she had a pulse."

A snigger went through the room. Jess could always get the others round her. They were scared of Lindy but they were a bit scared of Jess too. Jess used to be the leader of the Jayne family, the posh-girl gang, with Sarah and Emily, until Emily left at Easter. Lindy used to hang out with them sometimes. At least when they were all being nasty together she felt part of a crowd. But that didn't happen any more.

If I ignore her, she'll get bored and leave me alone.

"That's the trouble with the Bellows family," Jess went on, "they're all brain-dead. Someone should switch off their life support." The room erupted with laughter and Lindy leapt to her feet. She couldn't stop herself now.

"Leave my family alone!" she screamed and she poked at Jess's face with her spearnail, the one on her right forefinger, which she kept sharpened to a point.

Jess stumbled back, losing her balance, a startled look on her face. A gasp rippled round the changing room. Then Lindy said, "Where's the Jayne family now, Jess?" and everyone laughed again.

The door flew open and Miss Wold, the P.E. teacher, came striding in, basketball under her arm, Nike shorts and white vest showing off her muscles.

Jess turned away and Lindy shook the inhaler in the teacher's direction, but Miss Wold ignored her, picking her way through the mass of clothing scattered over the floor.

"Get this lot cleared up pronto," she said, glaring round the room. She caught sight of Jess pulling on her T-shirt. "Why aren't you changed? Thirty seconds or it's detention."

Lindy started to feel flustered. Was she going to have to say something? Just then the teacher fixed her with a suspicious look and snapped, "Where's your kit?"

Lindy shook the inhaler again.

"Note?"

"Lost it," said Lindy, her fingers pulling the frayed cuffs of her grey school jumper over her hands.

"So," said Miss Wold, her massive frame towering over Lindy in the crowded room, thick with deodorant spray and perfume, "asthma is it now? Is this from the doctor?"

Lindy nodded.

"I'll expect a note on Monday. Bring the ball out to the court." She thrust the basketball towards Lindy.

Lindy threw a smug smirk at Jess. *No P.E. today.* Clutching the ball to her chest, she followed the class out into the bright sunshine.

It was a boiling hot June day and the basketball court was a shimmering mirage of dust and heat. The class were put in teams and Lindy dropped the ball unceremoniously between the two captains. Then there was nothing else for her to do except slump down in the furthest corner of the court where there was a narrow strip of shade from a distant pine tree. Her arms were sweating under her jumper and her pale legs, which weren't covered by the shade, threatened to turn lobster-red.

Bending her head against the glare, she slipped into her favourite fantasy, the one where someone came to save her. Like Garth. Maybe they'd let him out early on good behaviour and then he'd turn up at school saying there was an emergency and she had to go home.

Nothing bad, just enough to keep me off school for a few weeks until I can sort things out, maybe even get away.

Or what about Dad? *Yeah, right, he's never out of the bookies.* Her list of saviours had narrowed to almost no one.

There's still Liam, a small voice whispered inside her head.

Where would he be by now? *It's only been four weeks, he can't have gone far, he'll be back soon. Travellers come and go, don't they? That's what he always told me.*

14

***

Liam ran the dodgem cars on the Island funfair over the winter. He'd asked her out one cold night in February and they'd gone to the pier in Southsea. After that she'd hung round the fair every night waiting for Liam to finish work.

She loved watching him lean backwards as he stood on the rubber runners, one hand gripping the pole, cruising round the battered metal floor, releasing screaming teenagers from pile ups. Sparks flew from the electrical connections above, lighting up the gloomy winter nights, and the smell of chips floated on the coastal wind.

Liam had long greasy hair and spots on his face, but he'd said he loved her.

Come back, Liam, please. I need you, Garth's not here. Dad's only interested in betting and anyway, he warned me didn't he? He said to steer clear. I didn't listen because no one ever listens to him and Mum's no use any more.

Liam had left with the other travellers without even saying goodbye. The lady on the candyfloss stall told her, "He'll be in Brighton, I expect, lovey. More money over there," and she'd given Lindy a free bag of candyfloss.

Lindy checked her watch. Twenty minutes until the end of the school day. She could hear someone calling for the ball and closed her eyes, willing sleep to take over. It had been

15

ages since she had slept properly. If she could just have forty winks, as Dad always said, remote control in his hand. But then again, if you sleep you can't keep an eye on things. Daydreams were all that kept her going now.

She imagined Liam sweeping down the High Street in a brand new Mini Cooper – she was always changing the colour, red was the current favourite – his hair newly washed and razored short, his skin clear and clean. Jess and some of the girls from school would be walking nearby. Liam would stop the car for long enough to let her in and behind her she would hear the admiring chatter of the other girls.

Then he'd drive her away to a new life, the one she deserved, and she would change her name by deed poll to Kylie Sophie James, the names of her three favourite singers, and she and Liam would...

"Dozy cow."

Lindy could hear laughter above her. She recognised Jess's voice as she squinted up in the bright light.

A semi-circle of girls loomed over her, Jess in the middle, hands on hips, hair stringy with sweat. Lindy blinked and tried to focus.

She could see Sarah next to Jess, all that was left of the old Jayne gang without Emily. They were rich bitches, always sneering at Lindy's family.

"Benefits Bellows," Jess would say and it would go right round the class.

Now Jess was standing over her with a crowd of girls.

Lindy guessed she was still furious about the row in the changing room.

Then she caught sight of a figure pausing just beyond the basketball court. It was a boy in her year, the retard who didn't speak. Their eyes met for a brief second.

Jess spotted him and called out, "Hey, Lindy fancies you."

The boy's head dropped, dark hair flopping forward, and he turned to walk away. Lindy felt herself begin to burn with humiliation. She fumbled in her pocket and pulled out the puffer, giving it a quick, practised shake.

"You OK, Lindy?" Alix Miller was hovering on the edge of the crowd, looking anxious.

"What's it to you?" snarled Lindy. She could see Alix's friend, titchy Kim, standing next to her. She looked like she was trying to pull Alix away but Alix wasn't taking any notice.

"Don't let them get to you," said Alix, jerking her head towards Jess. "Do you want to come with me and Kim?"

"Yes, run along with the kiddies, why don't you?" snorted Jess and the crowd sniggered.

Why does Alix have to poke her nose in right now? Always interfering. But as Lindy glared up at Alix and Kim, a bit of her was glad someone seemed to care.

Suddenly Jess reached down and grabbed the inhaler, saying, "What's in there? Bet it's drugs."

Startled, Lindy's head jerked up. Alix took a step forward and then Lindy saw, beyond the fence, the retard boy turn and it seemed to her that his face spread into a grin. A huge wave of fury surged through her. It was bad enough having Alix and Kim feeling sorry for her, but to be laughed at by *him...*

"Maybe he'd like some," said Jess, waving the inhaler towards the boy.

"Lindy will be selling at the school gates later," called Sarah Jayne.

"Yeah! Carrying on the family business," said Jess and everyone laughed. "I'm sure they'll let you share a cell with the rest of your family."

That's it.

Lindy leapt to her feet and, without thinking, lashed out with her spearnail. There was a terrified scream from Jess as blood oozed from a thin red line on her neck. The other girls screamed too. Lindy grabbed the inhaler, but, as she did, her sleeve came back, revealing the stained bandage which was unravelling from around her arm. Squeals broke out from the group of girls.

"What's that?"

"Yuck, blood!"

"Are you hurt, Lindy?" That was Alix.

Great! Alix! The one person who knows I do first aid. All I need is Alix Miller blabbing round the school about how I go to St John's Ambulance. That's no one's business!

But before Lindy could snarl back at Alix, Jess said in a mocking voice, "I bet she did it to herself! What are you, a goth? She's just trying to get attention!" She was dabbing her neck with a tissue and glaring at Lindy.

Mutters of agreement rippled round the group.

Oh God! I hate her. She is asking for a slap.

But Lindy couldn't risk getting into a fight now. Before Jess could do anything else, she turned and ran.

"I was right, wasn't I?" Jess yelled after her, triumphantly, as if she wanted the whole school to hear. "You freak!"

Chapter 3
Dead

Lindy ran out of school and along the back lanes towards her house, thoughts raging round her head. *My life wasn't meant to be like this. I'm better than this, Liam knows, Liam said he loved me. Everything will be OK when Liam comes back.*

At the corner of Gull Terrace she slowed to a heel-scuffing walk. She hated going home. Since Jemma, things with Mum had got even worse. She stayed at home all day, watching telly. They had never been close; she knew her mum preferred boys and Garth was her favourite. But now Mum didn't even look up when she came home. And there would be nothing for dinner again.

Why couldn't I have a mum like Jess's? Jess's mum always wore designer gym outfits, her glossy hair loose down her back. She'd seen Jess and her mum walking down the High Street, arm-in-arm, chatting and laughing. *I've never done that with my mum.*

Jess's mum didn't need a job because Jess's dad brought in all the money and drove a Lexus convertible. Her sister was in the Sixth Form doing A levels, not in prison doing time.

Why wasn't I born into a normal family?

They didn't even have Winnings Night any more,

not since Jemma. Dad's luck seemed to have run out, like everything else.

Lindy arrived home, let herself in and ran straight upstairs to change her bandage. But when she entered the bedroom, Sean was already there.

"Scram," she snapped, as she threw her bag onto her bed.

"I'm starving, got any money for chips?" Sean's narrow pointed face stared up at her, his head shaved close making his ears stick out and his thin frame appear slight and vulnerable.

Sean was always hungry but he knew how to fend for himself, turning up at his schoolmates' houses in time for tea. He had one of those appealing little faces that made the mums want to feed him up.

"Can't you go round to Darren's?"

Sean shook his head, "It's his big brother's birthday, they're going somewhere special."

All she wanted to do was get rid of him and have the room to herself. Lindy thought quickly. The fridge was probably empty and she didn't have time to go to the shops. She had to go and check the plants. It was hot and she couldn't let them dry out.

"Here, get some fish and chips." She held out a ten pound note. "Make it last."

"Cheers," said Sean. "Laters, Lindy," and he went off down the stairs at a gallop.

Lindy heard him slow down at the bottom, wheezing in the hallway. *His inhaler.* She called his name but he went out and slammed the front door behind him. With a stab of guilt, she grabbed the asthma puffer from her bag, pushed open the bedroom window and shouted down to him, "Here, catch!"

She watched as he caught the inhaler, took a couple of puffs and started to breathe normally. Then he gave a cheery wave and ran off down the path.

Nine years old and he hasn't got a chance.

But she didn't have time to worry about Sean. She had enough problems of her own. Lindy shut the door and pushed a chair up against the handle. Stripping off her jumper and blouse she inspected the bandage on her arm. It was coming loose again. Now Jess and the other girls all knew what she had done. Even Alix and Kim.

It'll be all round the school by the morning. Lindy Bellows cuts herself.

She could almost hear the chanting of her class. Suddenly she pictured Jess and Sarah arriving at her front door one day when she was out and pushing their way past Mum with some excuse. They would run up the stairs to her messy bedroom. Jess would pick up the razor with an outstretched arm, her hands in marigolds just like her posh Mum probably wore, her nose wrinkled in disgust. "Oh my God! Is this what she does it with?"

"Dar-ling! How can you bear to touch it?" Sarah would say, like a Desperate Housewife.

"She is so pathetic."

The pretty girls, with money and cars and proper parents.

Lindy kicked the wardrobe door shut with a crash.

What do they know about me? What does anyone know! Everyone at school was always sticking their noses into her business; the teachers yelling, the other girls sniggering. They thought they knew all about her dumb life, with her dumb parents. They had no idea how bad it all really was. No one knew.

And no one knew the trouble she was in now.

And what about the school retard, what was he doing perving round the basketball court?

"He's looking for a slap," she said out loud to her face in the wardrobe mirror. The sound of her voice in the empty room pulled her up short and she started to rummage around in a drawer for the dressings she had pinched from her St John's Ambulance class. Picking out what she needed, she laid them carefully on the bed and sat down. The empty cot yawned in front of her.

Then the thought she had been shutting out all day came flooding in.

Five months tomorrow.

That terrible morning at the end of January, Jemma had just turned two. Lindy woke up later than normal. Jemma usually woke her up well before seven, cooing in her cot.

8.21 was the time on her watch. No time to get Jemma up and get everything done before school.

I'll skip school, stay at home with Jemma and we can go to the swings after breakfast. It might be a Winnings Night; Dad said he had a good tip. I could use the cash to get Jemma that penguin I saw in the pound shop.

Sean was still fast asleep. Looking at Jemma's cot, Lindy had expected to see her baby sister sitting up and playing with her toys. But the cot seemed deserted. Through the bars she could see Jemma lying at an odd angle on top of TerryTed. Leaning over, Lindy touched her little arm.

"Jemma," she called softly, but the arm felt cold. "Jemma," she said more loudly and she shook her arm a little. It flopped back onto TerryTed, lifelessly.

"Jemma, Jemma, wake up!" she screamed in panic.

Sean woke up and said in a sleepy, confused voice, "What are you doing to the baby?"

Lindy grabbed the tiny body. Terrified, she started to shake Jemma.

More awake, Sean shouted, "Stop it, you're hurting her!"

Lindy stopped for a second and stared at him. Then she screamed, "Get Mum. Now!"

Sean shot from the room and Lindy was left alone with Jemma hanging in her arms like a broken doll. She could hear Sean's small fists thundering on her parents' bedroom door.

Heavy footsteps padded down the landing and her eldest brother, Garth, appeared in the doorway rubbing his eyes, wearing only a pair of boxers. "What's all the row about?"

Lindy couldn't speak. She just stood there hugging Jemma tightly in her arms, tears flooding down her cheeks.

Then everything seemed to hurtle into fast forward, sirens screaming, the race to the hospital, Jemma wired up, machines bleeping, and millions of stupid questions. "Two years, one month and three days," Lindy said when they asked Jemma's age. They pronounced her dead at 11.54 a.m. Meningitis. It had come on as she slept.

"Was she quite well last night, Mrs Bellows?" asked the doctor. "Did she eat her tea; was she hot or snuffly?"

I did Jemma's tea and I put her to bed. She was all right, wasn't she?

No one spoke to Lindy.

Mum was still in her dressing gown, staring into space. Then suddenly she whipped round and screamed at Lindy, "You must have heard her crying, you stupid, stupid girl!"

Stunned, Lindy just stood there, pain and fear wrapping a dead weight round her insides.

Mum started to mutter, "I checked her last thing, you remember, girl."

Then Garth said, "Lindy's only a kid herself," but no one seemed to hear.

Terrence wasn't there, of course. Out with his gang, as usual. He had never taken much notice of Jemma.

But Garth had always been around; he'd helped Lindy with Jemma sometimes, running her bath and making her tea. *So why did he go straight out with his mates and do that burglary? He knew he'd get prison this time. The courts hate the Bellows family. Garth got fifteen months. He even missed the funeral. Leaving me with this car-wreck of a family.*

And then, a few weeks later, Terrence really lost it and stabbed a boy on the High Street. So he ended up in prison too. At least the boy had been OK.

It was the foreign boy, Samir, that Terrence had gone for. Samir was Alix Miller's boyfriend. Lindy had tried to warn them about Terrence. He'd always been a bully. Maybe that was why Alix was nice to Lindy in school sometimes.

After Jemma, Mum didn't get dressed any more and eventually she lost her cleaning job at the school. Blamed herself, Dad said. But she wouldn't talk about it, so Lindy couldn't tell anyone how *she* felt either.

Dad was much the same after Jemma, except sometimes he seemed to be in some sort of daze, wandering around the house, staring into the boys' empty bedroom. He still spent most of the day down the bookies. So no change there.

Lindy had started to realise how important Garth had been to the family. Fifteen months. She couldn't believe it. Going home every day after school felt like walking into a great gaping hole. Mum didn't speak to her, Dad was useless and Sean was becoming more and more of a nuisance, always nagging her about food.

If Garth was here he'd have cheered Mum up, taken Dad down the pub, got Sean to stop whining. What am I supposed to do now? After the funeral the cot stayed in the same place along the bedroom wall. Every night as Lindy lay staring through the bars into the emptiness where Jemma had been, she thought to herself, *It's my fault, all my fault.*

26

The page with Hamlet's words lay under her pillow. 'Then it started like a guilty thing.' She couldn't bring herself to throw it away. The English teacher had said to her, "If you worked a bit harder, Lindy Bellows, you could make something of yourself, not like those brothers of yours." What was the point now?

Lindy sighed deeply and picked some fluff from the little pillow in the cot. Then she carefully unpeeled the bandage. An angry red wound appeared on the inside of her arm. She stared at it numbly for a minute, remembering the moment when she had cut herself the day before. The relief was so huge she'd almost fainted. The pressure that had built and built after Jemma, and now all the new trouble she was in, seemed to seep out of her onto the towel.

She had sat for ages letting it bleed, all the bad Bellows blood flowing out of her body, spreading across the towel like that rotten fungus they had on the bathroom wall. Some sort of mould which she couldn't escape. Just like in Hamlet's home, only his home was a whole country. "There's something rotten in the state of Denmark," they had read in class. Lindy knew exactly what that meant.

The English teacher's words came into her head again, "Hamlet was a spiritual refugee, all alone after his father's murder, not fitting in at home any more." *Where do I fit in, without Jemma and Garth at home?*

"Is it a Winnings Night tonight?" Sean had asked again this morning before she shunted him off to school.

"Who cares?" she'd snapped.

Since Jemma nothing had been any good in the Bellows' house. Lindy sat down on the floor and leaned against her bed.

Chapter 4
Winnings

The last Winnings Night had been just after Christmas.

It was a cold day in early January and Lindy had decided to skip afternoon school to be with Jemma. She'd worked out that if she skipped a different afternoon each week it took the school months to catch up with her.

No P.E., no Maths, just an hour in the park with Jemma and then I'll make her scrambled eggs for tea. Sean can go to Darren's tonight.

But when Lindy arrived home, Sean was leaping the stairs two at a time, calling out, "Winnings Night, Lindy. We got gigantic sausages."

Lindy felt even more pleased she'd come home early. *And we'll get some cash.*

She went straight upstairs. Jemma was just waking up and when she saw Lindy she called out, "Linloo, kiss kiss," reaching out her arms to be picked up.

To Lindy it was the sweetest sound in the world. She was almost always in charge of Jemma, had been since she was born.

Mum had said it was time she learnt what to do. "When we were at home in Donegal, fourteen of us there were,

29

and me in the middle. I looked after the babies from when I was nine. You're plenty old enough, girl."

At thirteen, Lindy had been delighted. It was the best present she'd ever had. Mum did her cleaning job, put food in the fridge when she remembered and otherwise sat with Dad in front of the telly, drinking lager.

"You know kids, eh, Colleen?" her Dad would say, a lazy grin on his face. "They take care of themselves just like what we did. Me stepdad kicked me out when I was twelve, didn't he Colleen? I've always looked out for meself."

Mum, her eyes on the telly, would say, "Sure enough we did and our Ma never knew where we was."

Lindy couldn't understand it. Why wouldn't Mum want to spend every minute with Jemma? She was two years old now and perfect, with bubbly red curls, which wound like springs down her little pink forehead, and a rosebud mouth, which she puckered up for a kiss. Lindy never felt as happy as when she was with Jemma. She'd planned the whole of the rest of their lives together.

We're sisters. We'll always be there for each other, through thick and thin; I'll never let anything happen to my little sister.

She'd have taken on the Jayne family and the whole school for Jemma.

"Bring her down sis, she likes a sausage, don't she?" Garth was standing in the doorway.

Terrence came up and flicked him with an old T-shirt. She glared at Terrence and he gave her a smirk back.

30

You pig. You nicked my radio yesterday, the one Garth gave me for Christmas.

Then he said, "Extra sausage?" as if to make up.

She shrugged and Garth gave them both a little punch on the arm. "Come on, Winnings Night, eh?"

"OK," said Lindy, and Terrence gave her a nod.

By the time Lindy had washed and dressed Jemma in her pink T-shirt, the one she'd picked out before she went to school that morning, Mum, Dad and Garth were in the living room, opening cans of lager.

At nineteen, Garth was her eldest brother, a big, lazy clown just like Dad. Always joking, never taking anything seriously and neither of them had ever held down a job.

"Against me religion," Dad would say, stretching out on the sofa. Garth would just laugh.

But Garth helped her with Jemma's bath when he was around and made sure Jemma ate properly, not junk and take-aways.

"She's a little tinker, sis, ain't she?" he would say proudly as Jemma's mouth bulged with mashed banana. Garth would do anything for Jemma. But he also kept Terrence in line and cuffed Sean when he was up to no good.

It was Terrence who gave the whole family a bad name. At seventeen he and his gang were notorious around the estate. When Lindy went to school she'd insisted her name was Lindy Minogue and even taught herself to spell it off a CD cover by the time she was five. Terrence bullied her whenever he got the chance. He never had a nice word to say to anyone, not even Jemma.

But on Winnings Night it was Terrence who did the fry up.

Dad had won a hundred pounds on the dogs that morning. "Biggest win since that ten pounds on the scratch cards last November, eh Colleen?"

Mum nodded and pulled the ring on her can.

"Here you are Lindy," said Dad, pulling a fiver from a roll in his hand, "and another one for Jemma, get her a toy, you know what she wants."

"What about me?" shouted Sean from the kitchen.

"Get back here, slave," yelled Terrence. "Dad gets the first plate, right?"

On Winnings Night Terrence turned from bully into celebrity chef, cooking the entire family, all six of them, his legendary fry-up. Sean was the willing slave, peeling potatoes, washing pans, running to-and-fro with the food, an old black T-shirt of Garth's tied round his waist like a French waiter.

"Best one ever," said Dad, as he looked at his plate piled high with sausages, beans, fried bread, fried potatoes, tomatoes, mushrooms and three eggs.

"Toast and marmalade coming up," cried out Sean, running in with a huge tray, which he planted on the floor in the middle of the room.

"Good thing we don't have a dog," said Dad.

"Don't need one with this lot," said Garth, through a mouthful of sausage.

"Here Garth, love, have one of my sausages," said Mum. "Too many for me, sure enough."

Why did she bother to have more kids if she only cares about him? I'll always be there for Jemma, she can come and live with me when I get married, help me with my kids, like a proper family.

But at least on Winnings Night Garth was home.

"Here we all are," said Dad pointing his fork round the room. "Proper family night in, eh Colleen."

"Eggy egg," demanded Jemma and the boys all rushed to dip a bit of toast in their yokes and hand it to her. Sean was the quickest and Dad laughed as Jemma grabbed the toast and stuffed it in her mouth.

"Right little foodie, ain't she?" said Terrence. "No one cooks like your big brother, eh tadpole?"

A rush of warmth went through Lindy as she stroked Jemma's springy hair. *If Jemma's happy, I'm happy. Everyone's a winner tonight.*

When Lindy had Jemma she was allowed to sit in the second best armchair. Mum was in the best chair of course and Dad liked to sit on an upright chair, at the little coffee table. "Hate eating on my lap, that's for peasants," he'd say.

Sean was sprawled out on the carpet playing with his toy cars, his plate wiped clean. Terrence had abandoned the wrecked kitchen and was eating the last of the sausages straight from the frying pan. Lindy knew she would have to clean up later. But, for now, Jemma was falling asleep in her lap and a cloud of contentment settled over the room.

Then Mum said, "Come on, Garth. Give us a song."

Garth ducked his head as usual and mumbled something.

"Now then, son," chipped in Dad. "You know it makes your mum happy, eh Colleen?"

"You've the voice, now, haven't you?" said Mum.

It was a tense moment and even Terrence knew to keep his mouth shut. Give Garth time. It was worth it. Garth had a voice which could 'soften the darkest heart', as Mum liked to say.

"Back home in Donegal," she told them, "Granda' would play the piano and we'd sing the old songs on a Saturday night."

Garth had once done a solo in junior school at the Christmas concert. As Lindy watched him out of the corner of her eye he lifted his head and broke into Mum's favourite, the old Irish song, 'Danny Boy'.

"Oh Danny boy, the pipes the pipes are calling..."

Mum always joined in on the next line, "From glen to glen and down the mountainside..."

Their voices fitted together, like Jemma fitted on Lindy's lap, nestled under her chin. Lindy buried her face in Jemma's curls and wished she could sing so that Mum might look at her the way she was looking at Garth now.

When they got to the bit which said, "...'Tis you must go and I must bide," Sean called out, "What's 'bide'?"

It was Terrence who answered, "It's Irish thicko, 'bide' means 'stay', the bloke goes off and the girl stays home, right Mum?"

But Mum didn't even nod, her eyes still on Garth. Terrence scowled into his plate, and Lindy had to admit she knew just how he was feeling for once.

The last bit of 'Danny Boy' always made Lindy feel so sad, when the girl talks about dying and ends with, "I'll simply sleep in peace until you come to me."

Mum leaned over and brushed the fringe from Garth's forehead as he fell silent and Lindy caught Terrence's eye for a second.

Then they all clapped and cheered, Sean sticking his fingers in his mouth and giving a piercing whistle. Jemma stirred in her sleep and Lindy hugged the warm little body against her chest, pushing down the empty feelings inside.

"You should go on the X Factor, son, eh Colleen?" Dad said and Mum nodded, a satisfied smile on her face.

That was the last Winnings Night, the week before Jemma died.

Now that line drifted into Lindy's mind again as she looked at the empty cot. She thought of Jemma. *I'll simply sleep in peace until you come to me.*

Chapter 5
Greenhouse

Lindy woke up feeling heavy. She'd been asleep on the bedroom floor beside the cot. It was almost five and she had to get to the house and do her job or she'd be in big trouble. She went downstairs and out of the house, grabbing Garth's old mountain bike, and set off towards Hayling Island. It was a good thirty minutes cycle across town and under the motorway to the road leading to Langstone Bridge. At least there weren't any hills – it was all very flat on this part of the coast – but she was nearly choked by exhaust fumes in the warm still air.

Once she reached the bridge onto the Island she slowed down a bit. Miles of blue sea stretched out on either side and little boats sailed to-and-fro.

If I could only sail far, far away. But she was trapped and anyway, where would she go? *If only Liam would come back.*

It was Garth who had got her the job. He'd sorted it out from prison. He knew how much worse everything was at home after Jemma. The note he'd written her on regulation paper a couple of months ago was still under her pillow. She thought it was her lifeboat come to rescue her.

Hey sis, I got you a job. Give you sum cash, help Sean

also. Cuzin Colin got sumthing speshial for you, just until I'm out. Garth xx.

Cousin Colin turned up just after Easter, like Garth said he would. Mum was all over him, even though he was Dad's nephew. He reminded her of Garth, of course.

"There's some cans in the fridge, be off and get one for your cousin, girl."

Dad wasn't pleased. "There's a bad smell in the house," he muttered, his face dark with dislike. "You want to stay well clear of him," he told Lindy as he went off to the bookies. "He's *proper* no good."

But Mum just said he was jealous. "You've made something of yourself Colin, sure enough, and *he* can't even get a win on the horses." She patted the sofa for Colin to sit down.

Lindy didn't understand what Dad was going on about and anyway, Colin was a bit like Garth, wasn't he? She watched as her cousin handed out Easter eggs all round the family. Lindy's egg had her favourite sweets inside and was sitting on a beautifully wrapped make-up box.

"Sort of a mini Winnings Night," said Sean, his face smeared with chocolate already. Lindy couldn't help agreeing.

Colin had taken her out in his open-top BMW, all the way to Southampton on the motorway. She stood up part of the time, gripping the roof and feeling like a film star as the wind streamed through her hair. They had lunch in a pub – steak and chips and half a lager.

"You look old enough, Linds," Colin assured her as he brought over the drinks and certainly no one challenged them.

In one short hour her life completely changed. Colin had a bit of a job he wanted doing: he needed someone he could rely on, and who better than family?

"Let's face it, Linds, your mob, they're either locked up or flat out worse than useless."

She raised her eyebrows and nodded, her mouth full of chips.

"You're the pick of the Bellows family, so…" Colin pointed his steak knife meaningfully towards her best pink top, "…you're the one I want."

It was the first time in her life anyone had said that.

She'd love to tell Liam. If only he had a mobile, she could have used Colin's Blackberry to phone him. She imagined his face as she said, "My cousin's got a job for me and he says I'm the only one who can do it." Liam would be so proud of her, wouldn't he?

"So what do you want me to do?" she had asked as she sipped her lager, finding it bitter but not wanting to admit it.

"A bit of gardening actually, cuz."

"I don't know anything about gardens."

"Don't need to. All I want is someone to pop round every day and do the watering. Just check everything's OK, you know, gardener, housekeeper, like. Someone I can trust."

Lindy nodded. She could certainly use a job.

I could save up and then go off and find Liam. He'd be dead pleased.

Her fingers slipped on the glass, spilling the lager. She glanced up at Colin, worried he would laugh at her. But he didn't. Instead he folded his paper napkin, very slowly, corner to corner, and dabbed at the liquid carefully until it had all soaked up.

Completely weird. She dipped a couple of chips in her ketchup.

But Colin hadn't finished. He dropped the damp napkin on his plate, took a small white packet out of his pocket and pulled back a flap.

Antiseptic wipes, like we have in the Ambulance. What's he doing?

Colin delicately pulled out a wipe and cleaned each finger in turn and then his palms and the backs of his hands, finishing up by wiping the cloth around each wrist.

He caught sight of her amused look. "Germs are everywhere, babes. People are filth, absolute filth."

She didn't know why, but a chill ran through her and she shivered.

At twenty-five, Colin was her oldest cousin. He had the sandy hair and light complexion of Dad's side of the family, but was shorter than her brothers, with a tight, compact body. He dressed like a businessman in smart suits and his nails were manicured. She listened as he told her he wanted her to go to a house he rented on Hayling Island every day, check all the lights were working and water the plants.

"You'll get forty pounds a week, two twenties."

Her eyes widened, "That's it? Just check the lights and water a few plants and you'll give me forty quid?"

Colin had nodded, leaning back in his chair, his small, round eyes weighing her up, a cigarette smouldering between his lips. "Every Saturday morning, if you do your job right." Then he offered her a cigarette.

She shook her head. "Lung cancer, learnt about it in St John's Ambulance. I want to be a paramedic."

"Silly cow," he laughed. "You stick with me, you'll make some real money."

Well, he wouldn't understand, would he? She didn't remember Colin at the funeral. She didn't even remember Colin coming over when Jemma was still alive. He and Garth just used to meet in the pub sometimes. But Lindy knew what she wanted to be. She wanted to help people who were sick.

After Jemma's death she felt so guilty, so bad for letting her baby sister die. A woman called Joyce came to give a talk about the Ambulance in school and Lindy went up afterwards. Joyce had grey hair and wore sandals and long flared skirts, even in the middle of winter. But she was OK. She even lent Lindy a uniform. Going to Ambulance classes filled some of the long empty evenings in the weeks after Jemma. Joyce was nice to Lindy, said she picked things up quickly.

I didn't read the signs with Jemma. I'm going to be ready next time. What if my Liam fell ill? Or Garth?

"If you work for me, you'll smoke," Colin said, mysteriously.

"Will I?"

"You'll see," and he gave her a little smile.

She was puffing now in the heat, the sun still bright, the Friday evening traffic already building up on the bridge that connected the Island to the mainland. Weekend yachters were criss-crossing the calm water and cars passed her with huge surfboards strapped to their roofs, music roaring through open windows. Carefree kids, out of school and college, were streaming towards the best surf at the end of the Island, filling up campsites and setting up barbecues.

If Liam were here we'd spend the evening at the funfair. He'll be back soon. I just know it.

Once over the bridge she veered off left and took the back roads between the fields. The house was down a narrow lane with a rough unmade road. It stood on a little plot of its own, surrounded by an overgrown garden. Beyond was a row of three cottages and then the lane bent away out of sight.

The lane was empty when she arrived. She propped the bike under the window and let herself in. Closing the door behind her always felt as though she was entering another world. The entire ground floor of the house had been gutted and turned into one big room. Long trestle tables ran the full length and every inch of surface was covered with plants sitting in deep, dirt-filled troughs. There was a green plastic watering can under the sink at the far end and a black bin to put the floor sweepings into. Colin emptied the bin himself each week, carefully tipping the contents into a bag and tying it firmly with a knot. He never left the rubbish out for the dustmen, but took it away with him in his car.

"Garden?" she had said the first time he took her to the house. "More like a flipping farm. Where's the cows?"

She knew what it was straight away but she didn't say anything at first. She wasn't sure what Colin expected. She'd started to sweat, although it was only April.

"How do you keep it so hot?" she said, gazing round at the room full of plants, already half a metre high. She started to walk forward but Colin grabbed her arm roughly, jerking her back.

"Look out, stupid kid!"

Shocked, she stared up at him.

His eyes narrowed for a second and she shrank back. Then his face relaxed into a grin and he said more softly, "You could trip on all those cables."

Looking down, she saw black wires snaking everywhere.

"Don't want no accidents, do we? Got to get the crop in, it's—"

"Skunk. I know."

Colin had smiled and said, "Nice little earner, Linds. Maybe we'll sell some to your mates, eh?"

Little earner! More like loads, he must make a big profit out of this lot. All the kids at school boast about trying weed at parties, the ones I don't get invited to. Everyone smokes it!

Terrence smoked spliffs and he'd offered her one often enough. But she knew what had happened to his friend, Jay.

"Some people can't take it," Terrence had told her. "Jay went mad, schizo. They found him walking naked down the motorway, his arms out straight, thinking he was Jesus."

So Lindy wouldn't try it when she was in charge of Jemma and since then... well, she knew all about lung cancer now.

Colin nodded at the huge, bright lamps. "That's what keeps the house warm. Cannabis plants like lots of heat. You mustn't let the lights go out."

He showed her how to change the bulbs. He kept a large supply in boxes by the front door. "Told you it was easy," he said as she climbed up onto one of the tables to reach a lamp.

Then he pulled two crisp twenty pound notes out of his pocket. "First payment today. Do your job right and you get the same every week."

She couldn't believe her luck.

Every time she let herself through the front door she entered a completely new world unspoilt by her rubbish family. Here she could plan, dream and be queen of her little empire. She imagined setting up home with Liam. Colin would let them have the upstairs for a little flat, wouldn't he? Liam could fix up a kitchen in the smallest bedroom once they'd moved the plants downstairs.

I'll ask Colin when Liam comes back.

Over the windows there were double layers of thick dark curtains to keep the heat in and she wasn't allowed a radio. But she didn't care; it made her green world even more private.

"Don't want to draw attention, do we?" Colin explained. "All them nosy neighbours. Think of it like a sort of greenhouse, Linds."

Lots of people have greenhouses. Maybe I'm even helping to save the planet. Colin doesn't use chemicals on the plants, does he?

"Our secret, eh Linds? Can't trust your family; you're the one that I want," Colin would say whenever they met. It gave her a new thrill every time. Colin knew she was better than the rest of them, he could see it.

It was too good to be true, wasn't it?

Lindy gave a sigh now and put the door key in her pocket. Her eyes felt stretched in their sockets from lack of sleep.

It was all lies; he was just softening me up, making sure I was trapped. Why didn't I listen to Dad? He told me Colin was proper no good and that's saying something in my family.

She pulled off her jumper in the stifling heat, the bright lights making her squint. Outside in the lane she could hear the putter of an engine, perhaps a small motorbike slowing down.

Wish I could drive away forever and find Liam.

The heavy smell of the ripening plants was clogging her nose. More and more she found herself feeling sick and dizzy in the house as though she was already smoking the skunk, dragging the thick blue smoke into her lungs. She began to wheeze at the thought.

Is this what asthma feels like? Maybe I should nick another one of Sean's puffers, just in case.

Surely he could get more, the school nurse would give him another one, wouldn't she?

Lindy mentally began to tick off her jobs for the day. Check all the lamps – two of them had gone; water the plants; sweep the floor, including the corners – fanatical Colin hated any dirt anywhere, she knew that for certain; make sure the windows are firmly locked. Sometimes she opened the bathroom window a crack, just to try and let some air in. But Colin would go mental if he knew, so she was scared to leave it open for long.

She picked up the watering can, wincing at the pain in her arm and was about to run the water in the sink when she heard a noise. A little scratching sound was coming from upstairs. She froze, hand poised over the tap, mouth open, ears straining. But there was nothing, just the deafening silence of the house.

Now you're imagining stuff. But Lindy stood for a minute staring at the front door. Then, not wanting Colin to find her like that, she trudged reluctantly up the stairs, stopping to listen halfway.

As she reached the landing and walked towards the bathroom she heard a single, heavy thud. A deep dread swept through her as she peered through the doorway.

It wasn't Colin.

The weird, dumb boy from school who had laughed at her on the basketball court stood on the bare boards, hair flopping forward, and in his right hand was a knife, a proper blade, not a sharpened fingernail.

Oh my God! He's mad. And he's going to kill me.

Chapter 6
Coke

The boy stood staring at her. Lindy could now see that the knife was just a penknife. She watched as he carefully closed the blade and slid it into the pocket of his black jeans. His feet were encased in thick boots with chains at the heels, which explained the thud, and he wore a black T-shirt that read in white goth letters, 'Do Not Resuscitate'. Shaggy black hair hung down below his ears and surprisingly bushy eyebrows almost met in the middle of his forehead. His eyebrows were quite cute.

"How did you get in here?" she yelled, suddenly angry now she knew he wasn't going to stab her.

The boy stared at her blankly.

"Who do you think you are, James Bond?"

Same blank stare. Lindy was getting really mad now. She said in a louder voice, "You want to rob us? You must be mad, there's nothing in here, you muppet."

The boy didn't answer, just turned and pointed. To Lindy's amazement she saw that a whole pane of glass had been removed from the window and was propped neatly under the sink.

"You took that out?"

He nodded.

"To get in here?"

He nodded again.

"Why?"

The boy just stood there.

This is getting boring. And he's in the Special Unit, isn't he? That's for kids who are dumb.

He was almost the same height as her, but quite thin and droopy. *Maybe he's on drugs.*

"You can't stay here."

The boy pushed past her and, dodging along the corridor, ran lightly down the stairs.

"Hey! Where are you going?" She ran after him, her feet thumping on the uncarpeted staircase. He was walking between the plants and was reaching out to touch them.

"Pack that in!" she called out as she got to the bottom of the stairs. "And watch the wires." But he ignored her. *Is he deaf as well as dumb?*

Running over she grabbed his arm and forced him round to face her. "Watch my lips," she shouted. "Don't trip on the wires." She waved her hands over the floor and shook her head hard. "You'll get me into trouble."

The boy's face changed quite slowly and deliberately. His eyebrows met in a thick line, dark eyes staring at her. Then he pulled his arm away, put his hands in his pockets, lowered his head and levered his shoulders up and then down slowly. It was as if he was saying sorry.

"So not deaf and not quite so dumb."

They stood opposite each other, the boy's face impassive

48

in the heavy silence of the house. Lindy imagined Colin's fury at finding them there together.

She laughed a little to break the silence and then said in a too-bright voice, "Colin's my cousin. Cous-in. Right?"

Quick nod.

She continued speaking slowly, "If Colin comes in and sees you, I don't know what he'd… well, you know, it's his house. I just look after the plants."

No reaction.

A thought occurred to her. She pointed to herself and said, "Lindy. Lin-dy."

The boy stared at her for a few seconds. Then he took a pen out of his pocket and wrote on the palm of his hand: KARL.

He really doesn't speak at all. She felt the tight muscles in her neck and shoulders relax. If he doesn't speak, he can't tell.

She looked around the room and back at Karl. She couldn't read his face. Did he realise what sort of place he was in? Better if he didn't really and it was quite nice having someone else with her, other than Colin.

She folded her arms and stared at him for a long minute and then she said, "I have to water the plants and check the lamps," as if it was the most normal thing in the world.

Karl didn't react.

"Insane, isn't it, all this fuss over some stupid plants."

She hoped he wouldn't realise what was really going on in the greenhouse. Even if he couldn't speak, he might go and get the police. Then everything would crash down and she would be left alone, in charge and accused. But for now, it was nice just not to be alone.

She had only been doing her job for a few weeks when Colin told her his real plan. The cannabis farm was just a sideline. Colin was moving up in the world, and cocaine was his big plan to get rich.

"The first lot's coming soon, Linds," he told her one evening in the house, while she swept the floor. His eyes were shining as he went on, "You and me, we're a team, we'll go out in the evenings and you'll deliver the stuff to the doors. No one will suspect you, a sweet little schoolgirl in your uniform."

She found it hard to take him seriously. "Yeah right, what do you take me for? Cocaine? I'm not thick, you know. That's stuff's a ticket straight to jail."

"Too late for that, babes, running a cannabis farm can buy you a long stretch inside. And trust me, I'll be long gone when they catch you with this lot. You do what you're told and keep your mouth shut."

Prison!

Why hadn't she realised, why hadn't she seen this coming the very first day and just walked off, told him to stuff his job? *Because I trusted him, because Garth said he was all right. I should have listened to Dad. He said to steer clear of Colin, didn't he?*

She felt a freezing chill spread through her body. Her

knees went liquid with fear. *They'll shut me up for years. Garth says he's even too scared to take showers inside.*

"Garth didn't say anything about delivering cocaine," said Lindy, her voice beginning to wobble. "Garth wouldn't agree, you know he wouldn't."

Colin's eyes narrowed. He walked over and put his hands on her shoulders, pressing down hard, his face so close she could almost taste the stale smoke on his breath.

She began to shudder as he said, "Garth's not here, babes, so if you want to stay free you do what I say."

And that was the moment she realised she was trapped. She couldn't walk out and go home as if nothing had happened; Colin would never let her. But if she stayed and the police came, she didn't stand a chance. The Bellows family were famous in the courts. They'd pronounce her guilty and slam her in jail, just like her brothers.

"They watch you with cameras," Terrence had told her once, after he'd been held overnight in a police station.

"What, in the cells?"

Terrence had given a little nod and a nasty grin. "They even watch you when you pee."

Lindy was horrified. She would die if she had to sit on a toilet doing her business, with all the cops standing round the TV screen laughing at her.

"The filth can do anything with you once you're in their hands," Terrence was always saying.

I'm going to prison, I'm going to prison, I'm going to prison, swirled round and round her head all day and night. She couldn't sleep, she could hardly eat. She thought Colin had come to pull her out of her sadness after Jemma. Instead he had made her life unbearable and she couldn't tell anybody. Like Hamlet, all alone and no one to turn to, watching his dad's murderer laugh with his mum over dinner. And like Hamlet she didn't know what to do next.

If I told Colin I was a spiritual refugee, he'd laugh at me.

All the pleasure attached to her job and the private green world had died. And Colin became more and more cruel.

"Sweep that floor again, I run a tight ship here, don't want no infestations."

"But I thought—"

"I don't pay you to think. Keep the place tidy, water the plants, shut your mouth." His voice crackled in the heat.

Confused and hurt, she thought back to his words in the pub all those weeks ago, "You're the one I want."

He had made her feel so special, now she couldn't stand being in the same room as him. And the worst was yet to come.

Colin was already in the greenhouse when she arrived one evening. He'd laid out a twenty pound note on top of the electric meter. She watched as he took out a little plastic bag of white powder, poured the contents in a line on the note, rolled the note up, and snorted the contents up his left nostril.

Cocaine! It must be. I'm not taking that stuff. What if he makes me?

Colin loosened his tie, his eyes beginning to glaze over. Then he shook out the note and with a little smile, slapped it in her hand. "Just do your job, don't ask questions and remember, if I go down, you go down with me. Right?"

She couldn't speak. Her throat was rigid with fear.

"Understand?"

She nodded vigorously. Without another word he went out, slamming the door behind him.

After that she lay awake every night, staring at the empty cot, holding her breath, waiting for the police to come banging on the front door. The terror grew until she couldn't stand it any longer and she'd cut herself.

Look where that got me today. At war with Jess and her posse. Now this idiot could give everything away.

Her voice trembled a little. "Colin's very particular about his garden, God knows why."

Karl nodded.

Perhaps he's one of those super-intelligent kids who know everything and don't need to talk. Uses extra-sensory whatsits like people on the telly who read minds. Perhaps he can read my mind.

"Can you?" she said out loud.

Quizzical eyebrows from Karl. *Those eyebrows can do everything. Perhaps that's why he doesn't bother talking?*

"Can you read my mind?"

His face broke into a soundless laugh. It was really weird to watch.

"OK, so why are you here?"

Karl didn't move.

"There's nothing to steal in this house."

His face stayed blank.

Maybe he just wants to hang out.

She stared back for a minute, not sure what to do and then she shrugged and said, "You want to help me?"

He didn't respond and she turned away, looking round for the watering can. Then she felt a light touch on her shoulder. Turning back she saw Karl, a bit shorter than her five foot six, standing really close, gazing into her eyes. Then he slowly nodded and his eyebrows settled into one sincere-looking black line. For a minute she let her eyes meet his gaze and a strange feeling of calm swept over her. This was so much better than being alone with her fear and a house full of drugs.

Karl was a quick learner, pouring just enough water without flooding the trays. He could also change lightbulbs, levering his slight thin form onto a table to reach one of the high-up lamps. Lindy collected any dead or yellowing leaves and swept the floor.

Slowly, she began to talk as they worked. "Been doing this since Easter, three months now. My cousin relies on me, no one else in the family's any use."

Lindy glanced up to see if Karl was listening. He nodded seriously at her and opened another box of lightbulbs.

"He pays me, I've saved loads of money."

The truth was that she hated the money now. She had

started throwing it into an old shoebox under the bed each week and hadn't bothered to count it for ages.

With the watering finished, they walked round the house together checking the locks. The light in the lane was fading fast as they finished.

"I hate cycling home after dark," she admitted. "I stayed the night here once but it was creepy on my own."

Karl widened his eyes and pushed his front teeth over his bottom lip like fangs.

Lindy looked at him puzzled and tried to work out what he meant. "What are you? Frankenstein?"

He shook his head.

"Dracula?"

He punched the air like a footballer.

"Yeah, right, I'm not that stupid." But she was frightened there might be ghosts in the greenhouse.

Karl pointed at his watch.

"You have to go?"

Nod from Karl.

"You'll have to put the window back."

Karl stuck out his upper lip and raised his eyebrows as if to say, "Simple." Then he ran lightly upstairs. She followed him, expecting to hear the breaking of glass. But as she walked into the bathroom Karl was just pushing the window back in place. It fitted perfectly. Not even eagle-eyed Colin would notice.

"So, tomorrow?"

He turned and looked at her.

"You could come over again... Only if you want."

Karl tipped his head forwards and widened his eyes.

A little rush of warmth went through her. "Yeah? Really?"

Karl nodded his head firmly, gave a quick wave of his hand and was gone down the stairs, clicking the front door gently shut behind him. The next thing she heard was the sound of a motorbike. She ran to the front window and pulled back the thick curtains, but the lane was already empty.

No, couldn't be. He's only fifteen, like me. Too young to ride a motorbike.

Chapter 7
Retard

For the first time in weeks Lindy was looking forward to going to work. It was Saturday morning and as she closed the front door of the greenhouse behind her she looked round eagerly for Karl. No sign yet, but it was still early.

Will he come in through the window again?

She heard a tapping noise and rushed upstairs, but it must have been a branch on the glass. *He'll be here soon,* she thought, and she started on her work, humming quietly. *When Karl comes,* she kept thinking, *he can carry the watering can,* or, *When Karl comes, we can sweep the floor together.*

She took a brush out of her bag and, pulling her hair out of the band, brushed down hard a few times and then redid her ponytail. She went up to look in the cracked mirror in the bathroom. There were dark circles under her eyes but otherwise she looked OK. Should she open the window a crack? She peeked out behind the thick black curtain but didn't dare do anything else. Colin might come in at any minute. But she still wanted Karl to come. He'd just have to hide if Colin arrived.

As the morning wore on, she became more and more agitated, jumping at every sound. In exasperation she finally whispered aloud, "Typical!" and started at the sound of her own voice in the heavy air of the house.

Can't rely on anyone, except Colin, and I wish he would just disappear.

She had relied on Liam of course, when they started going out, after Jemma. He was her first proper boyfriend. All the other girls at school went out with boys the same age. But Liam was twenty, a working man. It lasted for nearly three months, until that special night in his uncle's caravan. The next morning he was gone. May 3rd. She hadn't seen or heard from him since.

Jemma dead, Liam gone, Garth and Terrence in prison. I was ripe for Colin to pick off.

She pushed the broom round and round the floor. She had finished all her work ages ago but Saturday was pay day. The money was usually on top of the electric meter by the front door, which clocked up hundreds of watts of electricity each week, but it wasn't there yet.

The walls of the house were draped with cables and wires."Catch fire, catch fire," she whispered to herself like an incantation. "Burn the house down, set me free." But there was not so much as a stray spark.

She was dragging the broom under one of the trestle tables when she heard the key in the lock. It was Colin. Karl would have knocked or come through the bathroom. Straightening up automatically, she brushed her hair out of her eyes. She was wearing a tight black mini-skirt, a grey long sleeve T-shirt with a sparkly red heart on the front and her feet were pushed into black pumps. Colin didn't like her to look a mess.

"That's my girl, hard at it," Colin had a mean smile playing around his thin lips.

She smiled back nervously.

"Any callers?" he asked.

She had to struggle not to show her alarm. What did he mean? He never asked her that. Had someone seen Karl and said something to Colin?

"No one ever comes here do they, Col?" she muttered back, pushing the broom under a table.

"Just testing, babes."

Lindy said nothing.

Colin wandered among the plants, feeling the leaves gently. He plucked one, smelt it and rubbed it between his fingers. "This little lot will be ready soon. Then the real work starts."

"What do you mean, the real work? I'll be finished in here won't I?"

"Finished? You've only just started. Got to get the crop in. Lotta, lotta money here. And the other deliveries start soon. Remember?"

As if I'd forget. She'd hoped the cocaine dealing hadn't worked out. Now she didn't dare to speak, just gave a small nod.

"Don't worry, you'll get your cut. Be able to go on a spending spree, that's what teenage girls like, right?"

She didn't want his money any more. She hated it.

But she muttered, "Sure."

"Good, that's my girl." Then, pulling out his wallet, he selected a big pink note. "Here's a fifty, bit of a bonus; plenty more where that came from."

She stared at it. She'd never seen a fifty-pound note before. Turning it over in her hand, she muttered warily, "Is it proper money?"

Colin laughed. "Yes, dead proper. Don't spend it all at once. Give little Sean a treat, like Garth said."

Does Garth know about this? Maybe he's been onto Colin? Her heart gave a little leap and then sank again. *Nothing's changed, has it? I've got to find a way out of here and soon.*

Colin gave Lindy a few instructions about the plants, although she was hardly listening, and then he was gone.

It was Saturday morning, her work was done and she had fifty pounds in her pocket. *Right, I'm off.* Locking up the house she went to find Garth's bike. She had thrown it down near the gate and now to her fury she could see that the front tyre was flat as a pancake. But she also felt angry with herself for expecting Karl to turn up at the house.

If only Liam were here he'd fix the puncture in a second. Good with his hands is my Liam.

"Useless!" she yelled and kicked the bike. Gravel and dust flew up and some went in her eye, almost blinding her. Dabbing it with her finger, one eye screwed up, she could hear the sound of a motorbike getting closer and closer. Then the engine cut out and, squinting round, she saw

Karl sitting astride an electric-blue machine, arms folded, a smile on his face.

"What are you grinning at?" Her eyes stung painfully.

Karl pointed to his eye.

"Well done. I've got something in my eye." She turned away, trying to wipe away the dirt with her finger.

Karl appeared in front of her, holding out a clean tissue.

Weird, a boy who carries clean tissues. But then everything about Karl was weird.

"Where'd you nick that from?" she said, taking the tissue and nodding back towards the motorbike.

Karl shrugged and bent down to look at the flat tyre. His long slender fingers, which had been so helpful in the house yesterday, gently prodded the flabby rubber. For a fleeting moment she thought he would magically fix it but he stood up, shaking his head.

"Speak, can't you, you retard!" Ignoring his hurt look, she went on. "Now I'll have to walk all the way home. Its miles." Her eyes were still watering as she dragged the bike up and propped it against the fence. In the midday sun, after a morning in the sticky atmosphere of the house, she felt hot and sweaty.

I hate walking across the bridge, the cars drive so close. And how am I going to manage the job now without Garth's bike?

She felt close to tears and snapped at Karl, "Get lost." Then she set off down the lane, her pumps slipping on the rough track.

Behind her, the motorbike coughed into life and she could hear the low putter of the engine. Karl drew up, his feet scooting along the ground to keep his balance. Lindy ignored him. They continued like this past several cottages and a field with an old horse drinking from a trough.

Lindy stopped and rubbed her eye with the remains of the tissue. Karl stopped alongside her and for a minute she stared in the direction of Langstone Bridge, wondering when the next bus was due. She still had the fifty-pounds in her pocket. She didn't want Colin's filthy, illegal money, but, right at this moment, she didn't care where it came from. She knew exactly what she wanted; a pair of Heeleys, those trainers with tiny wheels in the heel. She didn't care they were meant for little kids. *If I was just a kid, like Sean, no one would bother with me. Colin wouldn't have me trapped, Mum wouldn't have blamed me for Jemma's death, I could just play with Sean and...*

Karl revved the bike a couple of times, breaking into her thoughts. Lindy ignored him. Then suddenly he laid his hand on her shoulder and something about the touch of his cool palm calmed her. When she turned Karl was staring into her face. Then he gently took a stray strand of her hair and looped it behind her ear.

Lindy reached out and pulled her hair out of its elastic band and started to pull it back into a tight pony tail but Karl reached out with one hand and stopped her, giving a quick shake of his head.

"You want me to leave it loose?"

Karl nodded and she shook her hair out. It was almost the same colour as Jemma's, but a duller red and more curly. It reached her shoulders when she left it loose. No one, not even Liam, had ever noticed her hair.

They were quite close now, Karl balancing on his bike and she could hear his breathing. The slogan on his T-shirt read, 'The Rules Don't Apply To Me.'

What does he really understand? If you can hear but you can't speak, can you be properly intelligent?

Then Karl suddenly jumped down from his bike, the chains jingling on his black boots and, giving a wave like a knight of the realm, bowed towards her and pointed at the leather seat.

Lindy couldn't help letting out a laugh. "You're mad! What're you saying? You want me to get on that thing?"

Karl nodded.

"Yeah right, I'm not completely suicidal."

Karl gave her a quizzical look.

Suddenly curious, she said, "Did you follow me to the house yesterday?"

Karl's face didn't change.

"And why break in? It wasn't to steal anything, was it?"

Karl shook his head and lowered his eyes.

She thought for a minute and then she said, "Just to prove you could?"

A swift nod from Karl and then a shy smile. He looked like a sweet child standing there with his thick eyebrows level. She felt something flutter inside her.

With arms folded and a mock frown on her face she said, "So you follow me, break into the house and now you expect me to get on your – probably stolen – motorbike?"

Karl nodded. He had that cute look on his face again and she couldn't help smiling.

"Fifteen and you can ride a motorbike without smashing my head in?"

Karl shrugged, then climbed onto the bike and waited.

God, why not? I'm sick of everything, I might as well get on his stupid bike.

"OK," she said abruptly. Then she swung her leg over the seat, grabbed Karl's narrow waist and they took off down the back lanes of the Island.

Now neither of us can speak. Maybe I should stop speaking too. No one would notice. I can't talk to Liam anyway, and what can I say to Colin?

She didn't like to think of what she couldn't say to him, so putting everything out of her mind she closed her eyes, leaned her head against Karl's thin shoulders, and slipped into a fantasy about riding pillion all the way to Spain.

Chapter 8
100 cc

It was wonderful cruising along the winding lanes, the warm air on her skin, her hair blowing out behind her. She felt as though she was flying. At the bottom of the Island they turned onto the beach road. Ahead she could see the sea, and in the distance the outline of the Isle of Wight, white cliffs sharp in the clear morning air. On Hayling beach, day-trippers were paddling in the shallows and walking along the seafront, licking ice creams. Wind surfers zigzagged along the shoreline, while much further out were the white sails of yachts on the open water of the Solent.

She realised that Karl was heading towards the ferry. Maybe he wanted to go across to Southsea. *We could go to the Mall, I know what I want.* But the thought made her feel hot with embarrassment. What would Karl say? *He won't say anything.*

They arrived just as the ferry was pulling in. Karl stopped the bike and they got off, joining the queue behind a man with a dog and a middle-aged couple holding hands.

"Do they take motorbikes?" she asked Karl in a low voice, but he just bent his head and pushed his bike slowly up the ramp.

The ferryman had white hair sticking out from under a

peaked cap. "You bringing that on?" he called. Karl nodded his head still low. "I'll just charge you for a bicycle, son. Two pound fifty for you, and two quid for your girlfriend. That's return, mind you."

Karl's head dipped even lower and he handed over a five-pound note. As the ferryman handed back the change he joked to the man with the dog, "How long since you rode a bike, Joe?"

"Right little Hell's Angels, ain't they?" said Joe, picking up his dog, and both men grinned. The middle-aged couple looked round and smiled too.

As Karl pulled the bike onto its stand and the boat engine started up, Lindy went to the side of the ferry and leaned over, looking down into the water. It was only a few minutes to the other side, but on the way the ferryman pulled alongside a small motor launch and Joe called out, "Thanks mate, see you about five." As the two boats bobbed and collided gently in the slight swell, Joe levered himself onto the other deck still holding his dog. The movement of the boats made Lindy feel slightly sick and she glanced over at Karl. He was staring at the horizon.

Does he think in proper words? And then when he wants to say them, nothing comes out? Or does he not even think with words? Does he not know how to talk? But he's not stupid. You can't take out panes of glass, break into houses and steal motorbikes if your brain cells are limited.

They reached the other side just as two fishermen were starting up their launch. The smell of diesel and fish hung in the air. Karl let the couple go first and then pushed his bike onto the wharf.

They walked across the wooden bridge and onto the rough road. A houseboat stood on the shingle spit, facing a small marina filled with yachts. It looked deserted. *Perhaps the owners live abroad. Perhaps they've gone away for ever. We could break in. No one would notice round here; we could be squatters.*

Karl tugged at her sleeve.

"What?"

Karl pointed to the bike and waved his hand vaguely about in front of them.

Lindy shrugged. "Up to you," she said.

They got back on the bike and drove off, winding through the back streets to Southsea front where the sea stretched ahead to a clear blue horizon. The wide road allowed Karl to zigzag joyfully for a few seconds. Then, before she could get really scared, he knocked back into a slower speed, the engine vibrating beneath them.

Lindy saw the pier ahead. Karl lifted his hand and pointed.

"Yes," she called in his ear and he turned the bike into the kerb, pulling up just before the steps.

He parked the bike and then they stood looking around, not sure what to do now that the journey was over. Karl was so silent, wasn't he, so utterly wordless. She couldn't begin to guess what he was thinking. It made her feel even more lonely somehow and suddenly Lindy had a terrible pang for Liam's arm round her shoulders, his lips roughly kissing her. "Love you, girl," he would whisper in her ear with his lilting Irish accent. At least Liam spoke sometimes.

Who loves me now? Jemma loved me and she's gone too. A feeling of hopelessness washed over Lindy like a cold wave from the sea.

Then Karl put his hand lightly on her arm and nodded towards an ice-cream van. His eyebrows were raised above those serious dark brown eyes. She nodded. *We're here now, might as well.*

It was fascinating to watch Karl. Walking up to the kiosk, he bobbed on his heels until he caught the eye of the lady serving.

"Yes, lovey, what can I do for you on this lovely Saturday morning?"

Karl pointed to the picture stuck up on the wall.

"Ice cream?" said the woman reaching for a cone.

Karl nodded.

"Just the one?"

Karl held up two fingers. He glanced over his shoulder at Lindy and she gave a brief nod.

Why waste words? Probably helps the environment if we breathe out less.

"Two ice creams, three pounds, and ain't we going to hear your voice today?" The woman swirled ice cream into the cones, at the same time calling out to a young woman who was sitting at a nearby picnic table, puffing on a cigarette. "See these two, Bianca? I can't get a word out of them!"

It gave Lindy a peculiar thrill to be twinned with Karl's silence.

"Can't say I blame them, me," drawled back Bianca lazily. "Load of twaddle most people talk. Only gotta listen to the radio. Whine about everything these days."

The lady in the kiosk gave a rasping laugh and took the coins from Karl's outstretched hand.

Karl smiled and nodded his thanks and Lindy, catching the woman's eye, did the same. As they walked off, Lindy heard the woman say, "Deaf and dumb, eh Bianca?"

"Poor little ducks. Count your blessings, Coral, that's what my mum always says."

Lindy caught Karl's eye and they burst into silent laughter, bumping shoulders as they ran up the steps onto the pier.

A smell of stale beer and urine hit them and pop music blared through the loudspeakers. The pier was packed with young families and a stream of people in wheelchairs. One of them ran over Karl's foot and Lindy was sure he would cry out but he just hopped up and down holding his leg. Lindy couldn't help laughing until they both collapsed on a bench, nearly dropping their ice creams. Even Karl was grinning.

Then a dark shadow fell over them and a voice said, "Enjoying yourselves?"

Before she even looked up, Lindy knew exactly who it was.

Chapter 9
Alien

Lindy gave a guilty start and her ice cream slid out of the cone and plopped on the ground. Colin's face creased into a grimace at the mess. Would he guess Karl had been in the cannabis house?

She glanced over at Karl. He had stopped rubbing his injured foot and shrunk back into the bench, tucking his chin into his chest. Colin didn't seem to notice him. Was that another one of Karl's talents – making himself invisible?

"Just out for a bit, nothing wrong with that," she muttered.

"Didn't say there was, babes."

His voice was sinister, making Lindy's skin crawl. She could sense Karl shrinking even further. Then she heard a shout.

"You coming, Col?"

An older, heavyset man, in a smart suit like Colin, was calling out from the pier steps. His coarse voice was so loud it bellowed above the sound of the Sex Pistols pumping over the speakers. He was bald, with very pale skin which looked almost ghostly. But it was his ears that caught Lindy's eye. They rose to strange eerie points on either side of his head.

He looks like a proper gangster, so creepy. Has he got

anything to do with the drugs? Hope he never comes to the greenhouse.

Colin raised an arm to the man and looked back at Lindy. His eyes were narrowed and he said, "I've got my eye on you, babes."

She shuddered and then he said, "Gotta go. Casino." He jerked his head towards one of the big hotels on the other side of the road.

Lindy remembered Garth telling her that there were casinos in the Southsea hotels but they wouldn't let him in. "You can't wear trainers and hoodies in there, sis."

Maybe Colin will try and cheat someone and they'll gun him down with a sawn-off shotgun. Isn't that what gangsters use?

She gazed up innocently into his mean eyes. "Have a good one then."

Colin nodded and strolled away, punching keys on his Blackberry.

She turned to Karl. His head was still lowered, masking his eyes. *What a loser. At least Liam could speak even if he only said, "Love you, girl".*

Jemma's tinkly voice suddenly rang in her ears, "Linloo kiss."

Tears welled up in her eyes and she remembered how Garth had said, "Every sad thought leads back to Jemma, don't it sis?"

It was true. This was an 'every sad thought'.

Determined not to let Karl see her crying, Lindy forced

herself to her feet and marched towards the end of the pier, wiping her eyes furiously with the back of her hand. The crowds got thicker and thicker and she was almost shoving people aside in her fury.

It'd be better if I just lose Karl, what use is he to anyone? He can take himself and that heap of junk back home on the ferry.

She scrunched the fifty-pound note in her pocket.

I hate him!

But who did she really hate? Colin, Karl, Liam? Definitely Dad, but what about Garth? He hadn't even made it to Jemma's funeral.

That had been a sunny day too, but so cold. It was the end of January. Jemma's tiny coffin was lowered slowly into the gaping grave but Lindy could hardly see anything through her tears. Dad's eyes were streaming, his arm around Mum as she silently shook. Sean kept asking for a Coke and in the end Dad had yelled at him. Then Sean burst into tears too. Terrence glared at the vicar as if it was all his fault. But Garth, who should have been there, was already locked up for robbery and possession of drugs.

In the weeks after Jemma, Dad went off to the bookies every day. Mum lost her job and stayed home. Terrence went out with his gang. Nothing felt the same at home and yet it was almost as if everyone just went back to normal. No one ever mentioned Jemma, and if Lindy tried to say something about missing her, Mum or Dad snapped at her, saying she had to get over it. Didn't they care? Didn't they miss Jemma? Lindy just couldn't understand it.

She could hardly stand anyone being near her at school. She had never had many friends but after the funeral, she couldn't bear to be near anyone. Didn't want to talk about it. She grew the spearnail. That kept people away. They were too scared even to tell the teachers. Pathetic!

I'm Lindy Bellows, Keep Clear. That's what she wanted people to think when they saw her. Even when she helped Alix and her friends stay out of trouble, they didn't all become buddy buddies.

I don't need friends. All I need is my sister. And she's gone.

What she liked, what seemed to help a bit, was going to St John's Ambulance meetings. Joyce, the lady she had spoken to after the talk at school, was really encouraging. She was always saying things like, "You've got a real flair for bandages, Lindy," and, "Well done for remembering the correct recovery position. You'd be a really useful person in a crisis."

Lindy would bend her head so that the others wouldn't see her go red, but she felt pleased. When she told Liam he gave her a special kiss, and said, "Proud of you, girl."

Suddenly she could see a whole new future for herself.

I'll become a paramedic in a fluorescent uniform, riding around on a motorbike, medical bag strapped on the back. Then I could save lives, couldn't I? If something happened to Liam or Garth, or if Sean couldn't breathe properly, I'd know what to do. Not like when Jemma was ill. I won't make a mistake again.

But now that Colin had turned her into a drug dealer, she didn't have a future at all any more, except prison.

Reaching the end of the pier she turned, bumping so hard into Karl that they both staggered backwards.

"Watch where you're going!" she said, and Karl brushed himself down as people turned to stare. "Oh, come on. Everyone's looking, let's get out of here," and, grabbing his arm, she dragged him back to the main road.

"So off you go then," and she nodded towards the bike, but Karl lingered and part of her felt glad. "Go on then, what are you waiting for? Christmas?"

Karl pulled the ignition key out of his pocket and offered it to her.

"Are you totally insane?" There was a pause and then she thought, *why not*? Grabbing the key, she strode towards the bike, rammed the key into the ignition and wrenched it clockwise. The machine jerked and spluttered.

Karl pulled the bike off its stand and stood there, as if to say, "Go on then."

"You don't think I've got the bottle?"

Karl shrugged.

"Well, if you can't even be bothered to speak," and, swinging her leg over the bike, she pulled back the throttle and revved noisily.

Karl got on behind her and she eased the bike backwards, scooting her feet on the ground. The machine felt heavy and unwieldy under her. She wondered if her legs might actually collapse under the weight, but somehow she managed to manoeuvre the bike into position, point it forward and then revving slightly, got them moving slowly along the sea front.

This is great!

They were approaching traffic lights and Lindy began to squeeze the brakes, but a huge column of bikers accelerated round them on Harley Davidsons. Wobbling furiously she twisted the throttle instead of pulling on the brakes. The bike jerked forward with terrifying power. She felt herself falling sideways, dragged down by the weight of the machine as it toppled over. She screamed and even Karl let out a grunt.

We've crashed. I've killed him. Lindy was looking at the sky. She tried to lever the bike back up. But it was too heavy. Then she heard some voices above her. "You're OK, man. Just chill."

"You get the little lady up. I'll grab the guy."

It was the bikers. They'd pulled over and come to their rescue. Karl wasn't dead. He was standing over her holding the bike, a huge rent in the knee of his jeans. Blood was trickling down his leg. She was already assessing the wound and planning the right dressing.

"The bike's fine," said a slow voice. She looked up into a craggy face, grey hair blowing in the breeze. "Chris," and he held out his hand.

"Thanks," said Lindy. The bikers were ancient but they obviously knew their stuff.

Chris nodded at Karl. "Just need a plaster on that knee, mate, and you're away."

He had a fatherly look about him and Lindy gave him a cautious smile. "I'll take care of the knee."

"That's the ticket. Just get back on, you'll be fine. Bikes are the only way to get around, right guys?" With a nod, the bikers climbed onto their own bikes and rode away.

Karl stood looking after them admiringly, his hands stuffed in the pockets of his jeans.

Lindy looked down at the bike; there was a dent over the petrol tank. She pointed it out to Karl who shrugged.

"Sorry," she said. "Perhaps you'd better drive."

They remounted the bike and Karl took off towards the shopping mall, parking in a quiet side street by a line of skips. Lindy fished in her pocket for the fifty-pound note. It felt like a dirty rag contaminated with Colin's stink. *Drugs money.* Did she even want it any more? She looked at the damaged bike and then, making up her mind quickly, held out the note to Karl.

"Here, you can repair the dent."

Karl stared at the note and then at Lindy, his eyebrows in a puzzled line. "My cousin gave it to me. For the gardening."

Karl just stood there. A cat yowled in one of the skips and a four-wheel drive Jeep with bull bars gleaming on the front eased passed them. The narrow street seemed even hotter as the high back walls of the Mall pressed in round them.

Then Karl took the stiff, pink note. He rolled it between

his fingers, so that it was narrow at one end, wider at the other end, like a cone. He raised his eyebrows at her.

What's he up to now?

He pulled a box of matches out of his pocket.

"Yeah, yeah. Big deal; looks like a spliff." Then a thought suddenly came to her. She grabbed Karl's arm and jerked it hard. "Karl! Do you know what Colin is growing?" For the first time she noticed how intelligent his eyes were.

He nodded at her, eyebrows level, eyes unblinking.

She had to be sure. Maybe inside that silent head was the mind of a three-year-old. What did he really know?

"It's skunk."

Karl's grey eyes were still unblinking as he nodded.

"You know, weed, ganja, hash...?"

She ran out of words and still his black hair flopped around as he nodded, staring steadily into her eyes.

"He's growing enough skunk for all the kids in Portsmouth. It makes you insane."

Look what happened to Jay, Terrence's friend.

Everyone in school boasted about smoking weed. No one ever mentioned it could drive you mad, make you walk naked down the motorway out of your mind, like Jay. She noticed more and more stuff about drugs on the telly since she'd been at the greenhouse. There were hundreds of secret cannabis farms, just like Colin's, all over the country. She'd had no idea. The police had raided two farms in Portsmouth just last week. Would they find out about the greenhouse?

The weed they were growing these days was so strong apparently it made you go psycho, gave you schizophrenia, one doctor said. That must be what had happened to Jay. Terrence said he was on a mental ward now.

The doctor on the news also said you can get cancer of the tongue from smoking skunk. She began to imagine all the kids at school with huge cancerous lumps sticking out of their faces and everyone blaming her. *If the police don't get me first, the parents and teachers will beat me to a pulp.*

What would Joyce at the Ambulance say if she knew Lindy was growing drugs? *Joyce would kick me out, school would kick me out too. Then where would I go all day?*

And she hadn't even started dealing cocaine yet.

But Karl didn't look even a tiny bit worried.

He knows. He understands. She realised that he must have known since he first climbed through the window. *And he still came back. He came back... for me?*

Oh God! That meant he was at risk, just like her.

"If Colin finds out you've been in the house, seen the cannabis plants, I don't know what he'll do." A frisson of fear rippled through her. *If you've got any sense you'll get back on your stupid bike and get away from me.*

But Karl shrugged and took a match out of the box. Lindy waited for him to find a cigarette in his pocket. But instead to her horror he struck the match and started to light the cone-shaped note.

"You muppet," she yelled grabbing his hand. "That's fifty quid, don't you understand?"

Karl stopped and stared at her.

"You can buy, I don't know, *loads,* with fifty quid, Karl."
It was like trying to explain ducks to Jemma.

Karl didn't react.

"Don't you know that's Colin's money," she muttered and
she couldn't help looking round nervously. What if Colin
overheard her? *He'd kill me.*

But Karl slowly and carefully lit another match and,
fascinated, her eyes glued to the flame, she watched as
he set light to the note and put the narrow end between
his lips. The paper smouldered slightly at first and then it
flared into a strong yellow flame. Karl waited until she was
sure his face would catch fire. Then he casually dropped it
and let it fall to the ground. They stood looking down until
it had burnt to a scatter of ashen flakes. Then Karl scuffed
the ash into a puddle in the gutter and the fifty-pound note
was gone for good.

What I could have done with all that money!

But Lindy realised that what she was really feeling was
relief. Karl had burnt Colin's filthy money and he didn't
care, he wasn't scared.

Of all the people in the world, it was Karl who had
appeared to rescue her. She wasn't alone any more.

Chapter 10
Wheelies

They ran.

Through the automatic doors, then all the way through the mall and up the escalators to the third floor, Karl always ahead, until, panting furiously, Lindy cried out, "Stop, can't breathe."

Karl turned and sprinted back and they threw themselves down on a bench near a kiosk.

"I'm dying of thirst," moaned Lindy, searching through her pockets for change. But Karl was already on his feet and came back from the kiosk with bottled water, two chocolate bars and packets of crisps.

Must get a lot of pocket money, Lindy thought while they ate. *The bike, burning cash, more cash in his pocket. Or he has a great Saturday job. Or he's a real burglar.* She sneaked a look across at Karl. His head was tipped back as he poured the last of a bag of crisps into his mouth. She wished she could read his mind; see if words floated in his brain or if he thought in a different way. *Like an alien.* The thought made her giggle and Karl looked across at her his eyebrows raised in a question.

Instead she said, "Got no money now, have I?"

Karl gazed at her.

"Can't do any shopping."

Nothing from Karl.

"We could go and have a look? Can't hurt."

Karl nodded.

Lindy got up, brushed herself down and led the way through the Mall to a department store she had in mind. They went up to the first floor. There were some ten-year-olds trying on Heeleys, skating up and down the aisles, hanging onto each other and screaming. It looked so much fun. So free!

"That's what I want," she muttered.

She looked at him, expecting a bout of silent laughter. *A fifteen-year-old girl in Heeleys? How dumb is that!*

But Karl just walked over and started picking out boxes. He held out a size six. She stared at him. He'd guessed right. And he wasn't mocking her. A rush of excitement went through her as she sat down, slipped off her pumps and pushed her feet into the shoes. They fitted and were white with a pink flash down the side. Perfect.

The ten-year-olds glided past and snickered between themselves. Lindy felt herself go red. Then one of the girls, with long fair hair loose around her face, pulled up and said, "Do you know how to use them?"

Lindy looked at Karl who just shrugged, so she shook her head.

More snickers from the girls and then the girl with the long hair said in a world-weary voice, "I'd better show you."

Lindy pulled off the shoes and the girl showed her

81

what to do with the wheels and told her how to turn corners. Then she handed them back to Lindy and said, "Go on then."

Feeling more and more foolish Lindy pushed her feet into the Heeleys and stood up. She felt enormous next to the ten-year-olds and reached out for Karl. Her hand found his shoulder and she began to move across the smooth floor of the shop. The girls screamed and covered their mouths with their hands but she ignored them. It felt fantastic. Like ice-skating might feel.

They went past a mirror and she saw herself, next to Karl's slight figure, black hair flopping into his eyes. *I'm a princess with my slave. He's an alien from another world who doesn't speak but understands everything I say. He obeys my every command.* She called in a loud, imperious voice, "Take me down the next aisle!"

Karl, head lowered, turned carefully, making sure her hand didn't slip from his shoulder. It was like having an obedient dog.

They wobbled precariously down two aisles and were turning back up the third when a shop assistant appeared. "If you're not buying, put them back," she said with a glare. Lindy glared back, but Karl guided her to a bench.

"Fun while it lasted," muttered Lindy and she sat down tugging at the shoes. *If I still had the fifty-pound note... No way, I'd rather go barefoot.*

She stood up and looked around for Karl. He was standing in the queue at the cash till, the Heeley box in his hand.

She assumed he was giving them back but to her amazement Karl handed the box to the cashier and produced a credit card from his wallet.

A credit card! How does a kid who can't even speak get a credit card?

Lindy looked round wildly, expecting the police to converge from all sides. But nothing happened. The cashier slotted the card in the machine; Karl tapped in his pin number, took the receipt, folded it up and pushed it in his wallet, just like... who?

Who in Lindy's life had any kind of credit card? Her dad didn't even have a bank account. On the odd occasion he had to cash a cheque he went to the Cash Shack on the High Street. Mum used to get her money once a month but all that had stopped since Jemma. Terrence and Garth always got all their bent money in cash. Sometimes Lindy used to search through the jackets thrown in the hallway to find cash for her and Sean to have chips. But money, before Colin, hadn't come her way too often. Liam had been generous, buying her a couple of cans on Fridays when he got his pay packet, but he was often broke.

Now here was this weird silent boy, who'd actually burned a fifty pound note and had a credit card!

Karl walked back to her, tucking his wallet into his jeans pocket with one hand and holding out the shoebox to her in the other.

Should I take them and say nothing, say I'll pay him back, say thank you, say no thank you?

She took them, gave Karl her best smile and put the Heeleys back on. Karl's face, breaking into a grin, reassured her that she had done the right thing.

"Let's go then," Lindy hissed, glancing around nervously in case she saw anyone she knew. Placing a hand on Karl's shoulder she set off across the smooth floors of the Mall.

I should get some new clothes, special Heeley clothes! The thought made her giggle and Karl turned and looked up at her. She half expected him to say, "What?" and realised that she hadn't a clue what his voice sounded like.

Has it even broken? Maybe he has a funny voice, like a squeaky girl or a robot, and that's why he doesn't speak. Karl gave her a quick glance and then turned his head forward again.

They glided on, weaving in and out of the passing shoppers, stopping to gaze into the windows of her favourite shops. Karl didn't seem to get bored at all. In the distance by the fountains she could hear music roaring out a snappy rhythm, and as they approached they saw a crowd of teenage girls gathered round some mini-trampolines with a young man giving an aerobic demonstration. "Nice bum!" called out one of the teenagers and then they all screamed as the man spun round on the trampoline and spun back.

She had completely forgotten about Karl and the Heeleys, she was so absorbed in the scene in front of her, when she heard a familiar voice say, "Oh my God, I don't believe it!"

"Get back to playschool or what. How pathetic can you get!"

It was Jess with Sarah and behind them was a crowd from school. Even Alix and Kim were there. Saturday morning and the whole of Park Road High seemed to be out shopping. They'd seen her on her Heeleys, her hand resting on the retard's shoulder. Lindy didn't know which was worse.

"All right, Lindy?" Alix called out, shooting a nervous glance towards Jess.

What did she care? Lindy decided to ignore her.

She thought about running off, but she wasn't sure if you could run in Heeleys. Alix might know of course, she was always running, training for some stupid marathon. But Lindy could hardly ask her in front of the others.

"So this is what you get up to when my back's turned," mocked Jess. She pointed towards Karl and shrieked in a high mocking voice, "What are you doing with *him?*"

Lindy waited for the floor to divide and swallow her up. Karl had shrunk away, melting anonymously into the crowd.

Alix called over her shoulder, "Ignore them, Lindy," but Kim was already pulling her away towards a sports shop.

"Ignore us," said Jess bursting into laughter. "You could mow us down with those things if you didn't trip up on the way."

More shrieks from the girls and to Lindy it felt as though everyone in the shopping centre was turned in her direction, the laughter threatening to crack the ceiling.

Lindy felt her face go hot with embarrassment and angry

tears sprung into her eyes. There was nothing she could do. Crouching down, she unlaced the Heeleys and pulled them off. She slipped on her pumps and picked up the Heeleys, shoved past the gathering crowd and broke into a run. The shrieks from the girls rang in her ears until she reached the big glass doors of the mall.

I'll kill them, I'll carve my initials on their faces and rip their eyes out, I'll set fire to their hair.

She heaved open the heavy glass doors and there he was, her shadow, black eyebrows knitted together, his mouth a silent line. He'd run off, hadn't he? Left her to face the crowd alone.

"How does a retard like you get a credit card?" she yelled.

Chapter 11
Money

Lindy spent the whole of Sunday in bed, pop music blaring on the rubbish radio she'd got in the market after Terrence nicked hers. Around lunchtime, Sean appeared silently, like a little ghost at her bedside. "I got you a can of Coke, Lindy. It's left over from Darren's party."

Lindy stared through heavy-lidded eyes at Sean's grubby face, summer freckles spreading across his nose and cheeks. All the family except Dad and Garth had freckles and pale skin. Even little Jemma had had a cute brown dot above her right eyebrow. Lindy used to kiss it.

She couldn't remember Sean being cute. He'd always been a skinny boy, with hard corners at his elbows and knees, wheezing, surviving on handouts and his wits. He'd hung around her more and more since Jemma died.

Only Sean had noticed when she stayed out once all night because she was too scared to bike home in the dark from the greenhouse. The next morning he was sitting up in bed when she crept in.

"Thought you'd gone away," Sean's peaky face was pale from lack of sleep. "Like…"

"Like who?"

"Like baby Jemma."

They had both stared across at the empty cot.

Then Lindy had said quietly, "I'm not going anywhere, Sean, right?"

But Sean suddenly grabbed her arm as she stood by his bed and gripped it hard, his nails digging into her skin like claws. Annoyed, she shook him off and snapped, "So stop bothering me." His face had crumpled and she felt so mean she'd given him a fiver for chips.

Now she glared at him, her eyes half closed. She couldn't cope with looking after him as well.

Can't he go round his mates and leave me alone?

She thought of the Heeleys safely tucked away in a box under her bed. They had made her feel silly and giggly, like a ten-year-old again, not responsible for anyone, alive or dead.

She turned up the volume on the radio, hoping Sean would take the hint and disappear. *When will Garth be out on parole? Maybe Dad's right and they won't let a Bellows out early?*

"Lindy?" Sean's voice was insistent.

She opened her eyes a chink and said, "Get lost."

Sean dropped his head and scuffed his tatty trainer on the carpet. She could see he didn't understand. Who did understand her?

My Liam, and he said he loved me. He'll be back soon, maybe this week...

Illegal

"I'm hungry," whined Sean. "Dad's out and Mum's asleep." For once he looked just like a lost little boy, not the expert wheeler dealer.

Lindy relented and, scrabbling under her bed, pulled out a twenty-pound note.

Sean's eyes widened. "Where'd you get that?"

"School," said Lindy sarcastically. "Don't ask. And make it last the week and, whatever you do, don't show Mum and Dad."

Sean's peaky face split into a grin. "Wish I was in your class." And then he bounded out of the room, slamming the door behind him.

He'll end up like Terrence and Garth. Bellows boys only go in one direction. Prison. I've got to make sure I don't follow them. How am I going to do that?

She pulled the covers back over her head and slipped into a restless sleep.

Then it was Monday morning and Sean was nagging her to get up for school. She heard him thunder downstairs and someone else came into the room. Lindy opened her eyes. It was Mum. Lindy sat up in bed, smoothing down her tousled hair. Mum never came into her bedroom now, not since Jemma.

"You keep it tidy, then, girl?" said Mum, nodding towards the cot. There was a catch in her voice.

Lindy got out of bed and bent over the cot to hide her embarrassment. She smoothed the sheet as she always did

89

first thing in the morning. "Sean puts his cars in there. I tell him not to."

Her mother didn't say anything, just stood in the doorway staring and then she gave a small sigh.

If she starts crying I don't know what I'll do.

But Mum rubbed her eyes with her hand and said, "Garth sent a visitor's order. He wants us to visit tomorrow. You'll have to miss school, girl. We'll get your Da to write them a note."

Lindy was about to say she didn't want to go when she stopped. *This is it, of course, I can tell Garth all about Colin and the drugs. He'll want to help me, won't he? Unless...*

She turned to her mother, "Colin and Garth, they're more like mates, Mum, aren't they? Not just cousins. You know, they go to the pub and do other stuff together, don't they?"

Her mother lit a cigarette and looked at her for a minute, leaving it dangling from her fingers. Then she muttered, "Thick as thieves."

As Lindy walked to school she kept thinking about what her mum had said. What did she mean? Did Colin and Garth do drug deals together? Maybe that was why Dad had warned her away from Colin. But why would Garth get her involved in cocaine dealing? He wasn't like that, all his crimes were stupid small-time stuff, like breaking into cars and houses but only if he saw an open window. Garth never got into fights or even threatened anybody. He wasn't the drug dealer type. He was just a soft, lazy clown, like Dad.

Well, I'll find out tomorrow, for sure.

***

There was a lot of pushing and shoving in the corridor before lessons and when Lindy sat down she saw a piece of paper sticking out of her bag. It was a note.

I'm not dumb. Dad gave me the credit card. He won the Lottery. I hate the money. Your friend, Karl.

The words, *'I hate the money'* hit her like an electric shock. They whirled in her mind through double English. How could he hate his dad's money? She hated Colin's money, but that was different wasn't it? That was Class-A drugs money. It was proper illegal, cocaine money, not just a bit of weed.

If my dad won the Lottery, I'd stuff a bag with money, run off and find Liam and buy him a big house and we'd live happily ever after.

Karl wasn't in her English class. She'd always imagined he was in the Special Unit with the thickos, but he didn't seem stupid. How could anyone hate their dad winning the Lottery? How much did he win? One million, two million, forty million? Maybe he is a retard.

She tried to write forty million in her notebook, but the noughts didn't look right.

"Concentrate Lindy Bellows and open your book!" snapped Mr Davies, the English teacher.

She glared up at him but started flicking through her book. She tucked the note back in her bag. She'd find Karl later and sort this out.

"Who could Hamlet trust at court?" Mr Davies was

saying. "He had no brothers or sisters and almost no friends. Then he finds out his uncle murdered his father. Read on, Jess."

"Oh villain, villain smiling, damn villain," raged Hamlet in the monotones of Jess.

So many villains in my life. Terrence always bullied me, just like Colin. And Garth got caught with some cocaine. Is that the connection? Are Garth and Colin dealing cocaine together? But Garth's not a proper villain. He's quite gentle really, a bit like my Liam.

It was the judge who took against Garth, Dad had said. Lindy was shocked when she heard the sentence: fifteen months for drug dealing.

"I thought it was just a burglary?"

"Well, that as well," her dad had said, "but he had some cocaine in his pocket, so they threw the book at him. They think we're all scum."

"Very good, " said Mr Davies as Jess stopped reading and grinned round at the class. "Who remembers what Hamlet's mum says to him about his father's death?"

No one spoke. Lindy couldn't remember either.

"Come on, come on," said Mr Davies impatiently. Then shaking his head, he said, "Turn back to page six, line seventy-two, read on, Lindy."

Everyone flicked pages. Lindy found the line and stared at it. "'Do not for ever with your veiled lids seek for your noble father in the dust,'" Lindy read out loud. "'You know it's the way it goes: all that lives must die..."'

In front of her eyes, clear as a film, she saw the empty cot this morning and her mother's face as she turned away. A wave of fury whipped through her. She picked up the book and hurled it at the wall.

A gasp went up round the room and Jess shrieked, "Bellows has really lost it this time!"

Everyone laughed as Mr Davies yelled, "Get out Lindy, go straight to the Head of Year. I'll deal with you later."

But Lindy had already grabbed her bag and she ran out of the door and down the corridor. She could hear Garth's voice singing the end of 'Danny Boy', "'I'll simply sleep in peace until you come to me.'" Tears started up in her eyes and she brushed them away impatiently. Swerving left she took the stairs down to the ground floor just as the bell went for lunchtime. Instinctively she was heading towards the Special Unit.

I hate them all, everyone's against me, the teachers, Jess and her dumb mates. The door to the Unit was closed. She pushed it open but the room was empty. She gave the door a kick and it swung against the wall with a satisfying bang.

I'm going to find Karl and make him talk to me about that note, even if I have to break his arm!

Then she felt a familiar light touch on her shoulder and whipping round came face-to-face with Karl, his eyebrows furrowed in the middle. A rush of something sweet coursed through her. *Your friend,* he'd written.

"So what kind of friend refuses to talk?" she demanded.

Chapter 12
Madness

The corridor was quiet and empty. Everyone had gone to lunch and Lindy could hear the faint clatter of plates from the dinner hall on the floor above. All she could think about was making Karl speak and answer some proper questions. She had a list of about a million.

"Come on then, tell me about all this money, if you're rich you can speak, your parents would have taken you to the best doctors, wouldn't they?"

Karl stood there staring at her, his eyebrows making a deep black v in the centre of his forehead. It was infuriating.

"Why are you in this dump if you're so rich? You can't like it in the Special Unit." Her voice sounded shrill and harsh in the empty corridor as it bounced off the walls. "Or is it because you really are a retard?"

Karl flinched and his eyes dropped.

Top marks for meanness as usual, Lindy Bellows, you cow.

Everyone called Karl 'the kid who doesn't speak'. She was the only one who said 'retard'.

This retard is the one who bought you those Heeleys. Liam never bought you stuff.

It looked like she would have to admit defeat. There was no way he was going to speak. She couldn't make him even if she threatened him with her nail. She didn't know what else to say.

Then a familiar voice called down the corridor. "Lindy Bellows!"

It was the English teacher, Mr Davies, and another teacher, Miss Wold, was with him, staring curiously at her and Karl.

"The Headmaster wants you in his office," said Mr Davies, exchanging a scornful look with Miss Wold.

Lindy hesitated, looking back at Karl.

"What are you doing here, Karl Reece?" asked Miss Wold.

Karl's chin remained dipped into his chest and Lindy felt a new flush of anger towards him. *All he does is shrink-wrap himself when there's trouble. Some friend.*

But can you blame him? said a little voice inside her head.

Mr Davies looked at Lindy and barked out, "Well, off you go."

"All right, keep your hair on," and she flounced off down the corridor, her spearnail and middle finger raised in a rude gesture.

"Detention for that, I think, Miss Wold?" called out Mr Davies.

Lindy ignored them. She could hear their voices disappearing behind her and she was sure she heard something about Terrence.

Why hadn't she gone to school over on Hayling Island instead of following Terrence and Garth to Park Road High on the edge of town? All the teachers hated the Bellows family, didn't they? At least on the Island, no one would know her. She didn't stand a chance here. The kids didn't want to be her friend because they were scared of Terrence. All her hopes of making something of herself had come to nothing. She'd given up by the end of Year 7 and it felt like the entire world had given up on her, too.

Then Lindy had another thought and as she turned the corner towards the Head's room, a wave of despair washed over her. *The other kids must have told Karl about my family. I bet he regrets even being seen with me. Did he really want to be my friend? Would he ever give me another chance?*

There wasn't time to continue these thoughts. She had arrived at the Headmaster's door and was about to find out what kind of trouble she was in.

She gave one loud bang on the door with the flat of her hand. The door flew open and the Head ushered her in. To her amazement Colin was standing there, hands casually in the pockets of his suit trousers.

"Ah Lindy, your cousin is here." The Head looked at her and Lindy nodded warily towards Colin, who gave her a big smile. "Your mother has been taken ill and your cousin has come to collect you." He looked towards Colin for confirmation.

"Not to worry, Linds," said Colin, "but Auntie Colleen had to go into hospital this morning. Your Dad asked me to come and get you. All right, cuz?"

Mum's ill! She was all right this morning. How could she get ill so quickly?

A feeling of panic came over Lindy. It was just like Jemma. Had Mum got meningitis too?

"What's happened? What's wrong?" said Lindy looking from her cousin to the Head. "Is she going to be OK?"

"Yeah, yeah," said Colin. He'd taken his Blackberry out of his pocket and was tapping the keys. He didn't look very concerned.

Neither did the Head. "Is that all right, Lindy?" he asked, shuffling papers on his desk. He wasn't even looking at her. Couldn't he see what Colin was like? "Are you happy to go with your cousin or do you want me to contact your father?"

Colin's eyes narrowed and Lindy shuddered. She couldn't risk making the Head suspicious. "Yeah, I'll go with Colin," she muttered, and she followed Colin out of the building to his BMW parked cheekily next to the Headmaster's car in the school car park.

As they drove out and onto the main road Colin said, "Don't worry Linds, your mum's fine. Got a job for you."

Lindy felt her whole body relax. She realised that she'd begun to shake. *Mum's OK, she's not going to die like Jemma.*

Then she felt a wave of anger as she realised Colin had terrified her on purpose and lied just to get her out of school. What next? Was she ever going to be free? The police could be following them right now. They could be arrested any minute.

"Cat got your tongue?" snapped Colin.

"What do you want now?" She felt scared and angry all at the same time.

"*Now!* Don't want no attitude from you, babes. You do your job, keep your head down and your mouth shut, right?"

Lindy shrugged and turned her head to stare out of the window.

Colin swerved violently towards the kerb and jammed on the brakes, throwing Lindy forward against her seatbelt. Terrified she cried out.

"I said *right?*"

She had banged her wounded arm on the dashboard and was shaking with fear again. "Yes, OK, yes." She softened her voice, trying to calm him, every nerve on edge.

"That's better. Now, I want you at the house this afternoon. My mate, Elf, is coming over and he's got a delivery for me. You wait there, take the delivery, I'll be over in the evening before dark. Right?"

Her heart sank. "Why can't you meet him?"

Surprisingly Colin answered, his voice gentler than usual. "Got to be somewhere else, Linds. And don't think I don't appreciate you, huh?"

He looked across at her, but, taking a leaf out of Karl's book, Lindy kept her head bent.

"Lotta, lotta money in this for you, if you play your cards right. You're part of the business now, babes. You'll get two hundred just for this evening."

What business? I don't want to be part of anything to do

with you! I hate your money. I don't even use it, you scumbag.

But as she stared into Colin's mean, narrow eyes, she couldn't help thinking what she could do with all that money. Two hundred pounds in one evening. She could make over a thousand in a week. *What if I did this for two weeks only. Is it worth the risk?*

She could open a bank account for Sean so he wouldn't go hungry ever again, get a proper headstone for Jemma – Lindy had wanted one with Jemma's photo on, but they cost a fortune – and then disappear for ever to Brighton with Liam.

She thought of Hamlet and his murdering stepfather. Mr Davies had said that Hamlet was consumed with a desire for vengeance. "What would you do if your dad's murderer moved in with you and your mum?" he'd asked the class.

Jess and Sarah had spoken together, "Shoot him!" and then had collapsed into giggles.

Hamlet wanted to get even. Now maybe it's my turn. But I have to be really really clever and make sure I escape forever.

"OK, I'll be there," she muttered.

Colin nodded and turned the car towards her estate.

"Laters, cuz. At the house, all right?"

Lindy nodded.

He dropped her outside the front gate, tearing away at speed, tyres screaming as if mocking her.

Garth had to help her. He owed her.

Chapter 13
Spooked

She had missed her free lunch now and couldn't go back to school because she was meant to be at the hospital. Fish and chips on the beach, Lindy decided, and turned away from her house, arriving at the bus stop just as the Hayling bus was pulling up. She ran upstairs and settled in the front seat. The weather was cooler today and the sky was grey and threatening. As the bus crossed Langstone Bridge, the Island seemed to swim in a mysterious haze of mist. The tide was out, stripping the mud flats bare and she could see small boats beached at intervals.

I think Karl's in triple science now. Or maybe they just do reading in his Unit. She couldn't help thinking about the Lottery win. What she could do with all that money. *Does he help his dad count it at night? Is that why he hates it, because his dad makes him sit and count piles of five, no fifty-pound notes and slaps him if he gets his sums wrong?*

The thought made her smile as she got off the bus and crossed the road. The chip shop was empty, everyone was back at work or school. A chill breeze was blowing as Lindy wandered over to the beach with her chips. It was after two; she would have to get to the greenhouse soon and wait for Elf. The thought made her shiver. Colin said they called him Elf because his pointed ears made him look like a pixie. Whatever, he sounded scary, and she wasn't looking forward to meeting him. *But what choice do I have? It's my only chance to escape Colin's clutches. Make as much cash as I can and then run as far away as possible.*

"You skipping off too?"

Startled, Lindy looked up to see Jess standing over her, looking strangely small without a crowd round her. A couple of windsurfers walked past in wetsuits, carrying a board between them, moaning about the sea mist. "Try again later?" said the taller of the two, and his friend nodded glumly. Jess stared after them for a minute and then flopped down on the beach next to Lindy.

Lindy rubbed her thumb across her spearnail and Jess glanced down and moved slightly further away. The scar on her neck was hidden beneath her school shirt.

"What you doing here?" said Lindy.

"I had a doctor's appointment. Mum said I don't have to go back in this afternoon." Jess looked at the chips. "I saw that kid who doesn't speak in the dinner hall. Karl, isn't it?"

Lindy stiffened, remembering the humiliation over the Heeleys. "Dunno, just saw him in the mall."

Jess started to pile up the stones next to her. She was wearing a short, grey, very tight school skirt, the type Lindy always wanted but couldn't afford, and a short-sleeved shirt. Her tie was knotted to finish halfway down her shirt and she wore a pair of expensive-looking pumps. Her long, sun-tanned legs stretched out in front of her.

Jess gave Lindy a curious look and said, "I heard the teachers talking about Karl."

"So?"

"They were saying he's gifted. He's in all the top sets. They called him a boffin. Wouldn't know, would you?"

She's lying, what does she know about Karl? But Lindy was surprised at how angry she felt.

"And you know what else?" Jess blinked her clear eyes at Lindy, brows perfectly plucked, pink lips slightly parted.

Lindy said nothing. Why all this interest in Karl suddenly?

"He's a millionaire's son."

Lindy's head jerked up and for a second their eyes met. Then Jess said, "I've decided to get off with him. He's deaf and dumb, you know. I'm going to learn sign language. Worth it, isn't it?"

"What makes you think he'd go for a slapper like you?" snapped Lindy. *Shows how stupid she is if she thinks Karl's deaf. She doesn't know anything about him, its just gossip. Anyway, what do I care if Jess gets off with Karl? He's just some posh retard.*

"You were seeing someone older, weren't you? Liam from the fairground. I heard he'd moved on." Jess looked at her with slanted eyes.

Lindy stood up and dropped the unfinished chips in Jess's lap. "It's none of your business."

"You don't need to be so touchy," said Jess, pushing the greasy wrapping off her lap.

Lindy stomped away up the beach, her feet sliding on

the pebbles. She could hear the waves sucking back and forth behind her and Jess's voice calling out, "Didn't realise you fancy Karl yourself!"

Stupid cow. She had to get to the greenhouse and there was no way she could risk Jess following her. A bus drew up and she jumped on. As she looked out of the window, Jess was brushing down her skirt, her glossy dark hair lifting in the breeze. Lindy thought of Karl, his beautiful dense eyebrows saying more than all the words people spew out put together.

Jess will suck Karl up like a hoover, con every penny out of him she can and then chuck him out with the empties. He doesn't stand a chance, the loser.

But she felt empty inside. *Jealous?*

By the time she let herself into the greenhouse it had started to rain. The house felt cold and gloomy despite the strong lamps. She stood for a minute staring at the plants, her uniform clinging damply to her body.

Then she heard a noise. A tiny scratching sound. Lindy froze, her eyes on the stairs. The sound stopped and she held her breath anxiously. Then, just as she relaxed, it started up again. She swivelled round and back again. It couldn't be Karl, he would have bounded down. When other people weren't around Karl was fearless, riding his motorbike, breaking into Colin's house, flashing his money.

Lindy was about to move when suddenly the lamps flickered off and then on. This happened sometimes. Colin had explained it was just bad connections. But still her heart missed a beat. The last thing she wanted was to be stuck in the greenhouse in the dark with that strange noise moving around her. The lights flickered again and she threw out a hand, steadying herself on the electric meter. She could feel it vibrating beneath her hand. It felt warm and somehow reassuring. The lights seemed to settle and then the flickering started again, steadily, on and off, in and out, as if struggling for breath. The flickering picked up speed until it felt like strobe lighting flashing round the house.

Something's in here.

The plants seemed to sway in the changing light, bending menacingly towards her. Suddenly it went completely dark, worse than the dead of night. Lindy let out a cry and covered her face, fear ripping through her. Footsteps started down the stairs and in the dark a huge shape loomed.

A ghost has come for me. Lindy's whole body started to shake and shiver.

"Make it quick," she whispered into her fist. She was dribbling, but she was too petrified to wipe it away. Her mind told her to run, get out into the light, but her legs refused to move. A deep throaty grunt came from above her.

I've made it angry. It'll cut off my head and stuff it in the bin. She started to moan Liam's name over and over, positive she could feel skeleton fingers closing round her throat.

A round, moonlike shape appeared across the room, and Lindy found herself praying, over and over, "Jesus, save me, gentle Jesus," like they taught Sean when he was in the Christmas play last year. Suddenly all the lamps lit up again.

In the harsh white light Lindy crouched down, eyes blinded momentarily. A hand leant heavily on her shoulder and she let out a piercing scream. The hand wrenched off and slapped her mouth shut until she thought she would stop breathing.

Something screeched in the road outside. She heard a harsh voice say, "Shut it before the whole street comes in."

The voice was extremely nasty, but it was human.

Chapter 14
Powder

Lindy felt her heart rate gradually slow down and she found herself looking up into the pale, moon-like face of the man she had seen with Colin on the pier. She could see his pointed ears clearly now. It must be Elf. He was heavily built with broad shoulders and his suit jacket was buttoned tight over a beer paunch. There was something heavy in his jacket pocket, weighing one side down. *He's got a gun.*

The man jerked her upright and took his hand away from her mouth, saying, "Scream again and I'll strangle you."

Lindy staggered back wiping her mouth. She could taste the man's sweat on her lips and it made her feel sick.

"You knew I was coming."

At least I was wrong about the ghost.

"You scared me," she muttered. "And then the lights..."

"I was fixing them," he snapped. "Got a problem with that?"

The look on his face was so menacing she shook her head quickly.

Elf jerked his head towards the stairs and she followed him. In the bathroom she saw what had made the scratching noise. Elf had been removing some of the plaster with a knife to reveal a large hole in the wall below the washbasin.

The hole was stuffed with small plastic packets. He pulled them all out. Each packet was filled with white powder. It was cocaine, bags and bags of it.

"Give these to Colin. That's the stuff I hid last week when the cops were sniffing round."

"Cops!" A chill went through Lindy. *And there's been cocaine in the house for over a week.*

"Shut it!" snapped Elf. "Don't want no fuss. Here's the rest of the delivery." He pointed to a large, bulging holdall sitting on the toilet seat. "Put it all together, give it to Colin."

To Lindy's horror he reached into his jacket pocket and lifted out a silver handgun. The tip of the barrel remained in the top of the pocket. "Don't mess with me," said Elf. The look on his face left her in no doubt. He'd kill her without a backward glance.

He pulled himself awkwardly to his feet and went out of the bathroom.

Lindy didn't move, not even daring to breathe until she heard the front door click quietly behind him downstairs.

I'm alone, she thought with relief and then as she looked down at the plastic packets a wave of utter despair washed over her. *They must have a street value of thousands. How long before we get found out?*

The neighbours might have heard her scream when Elf grabbed her. *People will soon become suspicious of this house with all the windows blacked out. Especially in a small place like Hayling Island.*

The police will come, maybe today and I'll be caught with the cannabis plants and all this cocaine. Colin and Elf will escape to Spain and because I'm a Bellows and the sister of Garth and Terrence, the judge will give me hundreds of years in prison and I'll never see Liam again.

Lindy sank to the floor, too weak to move, tears streaming down her face. It was no good. Her life was rubbish. She couldn't even afford a proper headstone for Jemma. How could she ever have imagined she could break free? It was cocaine Colin wanted her for, even took her out of school to do his dirty work.

He was planning this all along, wasn't he? Soften me up with the greenhouse job and then, once I was proper trapped, get me delivering to half the druggies on the south coast. The police will catch me, I know it! Oh God! Oh God! Oh God!

Her head felt as though it would burst with all the terrifying thoughts piling up like the mound of plastic packets on the floor in front of her.

Her fingers closed around the knife Elf had discarded. It had a cruel, sharp point. She lay the blade on the palm of her hand. *But I can't, I need my bandages and a towel and all my other stuff.* Her head flopped forward and she caught sight of the plastic packets. *I need my fix too.*

Sliding off her school jumper she rolled up her left sleeve. On the inside of her arm, above the wrist, was the wound from last week. A scab was beginning to form and as she stared at it she remembered the huge relief after she had cut herself, watching the blood leak out, taking away all the bad stuff, the rotten Bellows stuff.

Colin won't be here for hours, there's no one to see.

Holding the knife firmly in her right hand, she placed the point above the old cut and sliced straight across the bare flesh. Blood welled out, and she laid her arm across her chest; her white school blouse was stained a deep gory red, but she didn't care. All she felt was relief. She closed her eyes and let go and then there was nothing for a long, long, time.

Suddenly she heard a boy's voice crying out, "No, Lindy, no! Don't die, don't die…"

Who's that? No one she recognised. She forced her eyes open to see the familiar figure of Karl racing out through the door and down the stairs.

Can't be. She pulled herself to her feet. *Karl can't talk, let alone shout. What's going on?*

She stood up to follow and then she looked down at her blood-stained shirt. She couldn't go out like this, someone might see. Scrabbling about for her grey school jumper, she pulled it on and staggered downstairs, feeling faint and wobbly. To her horror, the front door stood wide open exposing the plants to any passerby. Worse still she could hear voices in the lane. Quickly, Lindy grabbed the keys, ran outside and locked the door firmly behind her.

To her complete amazement she saw Karl gesticulating wildly to an old woman standing in the lane. Lindy could hear words, all jumbled up, but definitely words, coming from his mouth in jerky gasps, "Ambulance – Lindy – blood – dying."

The old woman, who was holding a small black dog under one arm, turned to go, calling out, "I'll phone 999."

Just then Karl spotted Lindy staring at him and his mouth snapped shut like a crocodile. For a heartbeat they stood looking at each other.

Lindy grabbed the old woman's arm and snapped, "We don't need an ambulance, I'm OK."

The old woman gave her a puzzled look and then she broke into a smile and said, "This is Prince William."

Karl didn't react. *I've imagined it. He can't really speak.*

"He's just a puppy," the woman carried on, in her strange, singsong voice. "My last spaniel died – very sad. He was called Prince Charles. When this one goes, I'll call the next one Prince Harry. Your boyfriend said you were dead."

The abrupt change of tack startled Lindy and she glared down at the old woman, who was wearing a thick cardigan buttoned to the neck, a woollen skirt and gumboots despite the heat. Her hair stood up in grey matted tufts on her head and a large, crumpled shopping bag dangled from her free hand.

Just what I need. Some old bag lady. She looked round, suddenly scared that Elf might come back, or Colin. What on earth would she say to them?

"Anyway you're alive," sang out Bag Lady.

Lindy could feel her hand growing warm and sticky with

110

blood and tugged down the sleeve of her jumper. Her mind was a jumble of confusion. *What did Karl see? The blood? The knife? I don't want him to know about this.* She felt her cheeks burning with humiliation, but Karl was already withdrawing into himself, head bent, arms wrapped round his chest.

Maybe I just imagined it, maybe he didn't really speak. And what did Bag Lady see? Will she recognise the plants and give me away to the police? I've got to get her away from here.

"Time for a nice cup of tea and a bandage," the woman announced, dumping the spaniel on Karl who was so startled he almost fell backwards. She set off back down the lane towards the next house.

Karl's head bent over the little dog, shifting its weight in his arms. Lindy glared at Karl and whispered, "You've got a lot of explaining to do!"

Karl didn't look up.

"Well, come on then," she said and set off after the woman.

The woman went round a bend and into a tiny cottage. Inside, it was very shabby with peeling wallpaper and threadbare carpet. Karl and Lindy followed her into the kitchen at the back of the house, which was a jumble of crockery piled on every surface and milk bottles filled with wild flowers in various states of decay. A ripe, stale smell laced the air and Lindy saw Karl bury his nose in the spaniel's soft black coat, his face wrinkled in disgust. She made a mental note never to let him round to her house.

The woman started running on again. "Don't do proper tea no more, with little sandwiches and cakes, that was all before, when hubby was alive and sometimes we invited the queen round…" she stopped as suddenly as she had started and fixed a cloudy eye on Lindy, as if challenging her to laugh. Lindy glared back, but said nothing. "…only of course she never came, so we called the dogs after all the princes and there's so many of them they'll keep me going to the end, won't they dear?" and, pushing a couple of plates aside in the crowded sink, she filled a kettle and lit the gas with a match.

"You make the tea," she ordered Karl, "and I'll sort out your girlfriend."

Karl had dropped to the floor and was playing with the puppy. *Trying to make himself invisible, as usual.* But he stood up and began rinsing mugs in the sink.

Bag Lady opened a drawer and took out a creased length of bandage, some cotton wool and an almost empty bottle of disinfectant. "Sit here," she commanded, and Lindy, too weary to argue, sat down on a rickety wooden chair. "Daft button aren't you. Soon get this clean."

None of this stuff's sterile.

Lindy felt the light touch of Karl's hand on her shoulder. Then nothing seemed to matter any more. *So what if Karl can speak, so what if Bag Lady saw the plants, so what if the police come, so what if I go to prison?*

The woman rolled back her sleeve and Lindy felt Karl's hand tighten. She stared down at the angry red wound.

Now he knows how horrible and stupid I really am.
She closed her eyes as the lady bandaged her arm.

"Only a scratch," said the woman. "We'll clean that up and then off you go out to play."

She's insane, thought Lindy. She closed her eyes and she could almost hear Jemma calling to her, *Linloo, doggie dog*, but the sound of Prince William yapping furiously pulled her out of her thoughts.

The puppy was sitting restlessly on his tiny bottom while Bag Lady scolded him. With a cheeky yap he rushed up and down the kitchen, paws skidding on the torn lino.

"All done. A nice cuppa cures everything, my old mum used to say." Bag Lady was bending over Lindy with a mug of tea. The bag was still floating in the steaming water and the milk had curdled. Lindy felt sick and glanced over at Karl, but his eyes were hidden beneath his mop of hair.

He won't want to hang out with me any more.

"We have to go," said Lindy. Karl was silent.

Don't you get it yet? I'm the saddo girl from the criminal family who cuts herself with filthy blades.

"Call in any time, we're always here, me and his lordship. We never go anywhere, do we William?" The puppy gave a sharp yap and jumped up at her.

As they walked towards the front door, Bag Lady called out from the kitchen, "Nice to meet new neighbours."

Lindy felt a chill run down her spine. What did Bag Lady mean? Would she be constantly knocking on the door of the greenhouse to borrow a cup of sugar?

They walked out into the lane, Lindy still puzzling things over. "How much worse can things get?" she said out loud, but Karl didn't react.

Why doesn't he speak to me now, when he was talking a minute ago? What was it that got him started?

And then she realised. She pulled Karl round to face her. "Was it because of me you started talking? Did you think I'd killed myself?"

Karl's eyes met hers and the look in them was so tender and sad she had to look away. As she did so a new thought came into her head. *Is it Karl and not Liam who really cares about me?*

She thought about all those long, miserable weeks she had waited for Liam to come back, longed for him as her life got worse and worse. But it was Karl who kept coming back, it was Karl who stuck by her however mean she was to him.

Liam's gone, Karl's here, end of.

Chapter 15
Hamlet

Karl bent his head almost to his chest, shoved his hands in his pockets and started to walk back towards Colin's house. Lindy could see the motorbike on its stand in the street. She hesitated, unwilling to go near the house again and risk seeing Elf.

"Karl, wait."

He stopped, but he didn't turn to face her.

"Is this all a joke, you not speaking, or what?"

He shrugged.

"Do you think I'm stupid, or I'll think your voice is..." She tailed off.

Karl turned slowly, his face unreadable.

If only he would move those eyebrows.

They stood there in silence for a moment. Then Lindy went on, "I don't mind if you have a funny voice. Is that it?"

His eyebrows slowly shifted into a frown. She felt a warm feeling flicker through her. It was safe to go on. "I mean, if you had some sort of operation, or disease, or something to stop you talking normally, who cares?"

Karl didn't move, but his eyebrows looked so unbearably cute, she just wanted to reach out and touch him. How could he say so much without speaking?

Then he turned on his heel and walked back to the motorbike, the chains on his leather boots clanking sadly down the lane.

Lindy stared after him, wanting desperately to go with him. But what about Colin? He'd said to wait for him at the greenhouse. *But he won't be there for hours, not until after dark. The drugs can look after themselves, just for a bit, can't they?*

"Wait for me," she called out. By the slight movement of his shoulders she could see he was pleased, and she broke into a run to catch him up.

They climbed onto the bike and she carefully put her arms round his waist. He didn't resist but fired up the engine and took off. She didn't know where he was heading, didn't care. After the misery and upset of the last couple of hours, it felt so good clinging to Karl's back, cruising the quiet lanes of the Island, no need for anyone to speak.

They headed south beyond the surfing beaches and the funfair to the road towards the ferry. Lindy laid her head on Karl's thin shoulders and breathed in his slightly salty smell. It was as if the sea was in his hair and clothes. She could feel the pulse of his heartbeat beneath her arm as she gripped his chest and the movement of the bike lulled her. If she closed her eyes she could imagine they were flying, far, far away to a desert island where they would eat coconuts and she could teach him to speak again. *Maybe he's just forgotten how and he's chosen me to help him.* She wanted the bike ride to go on forever.

Then Karl swerved off the road and onto a sandy track between bushes and low trees. She hadn't been to this part of the Island before, but Karl seemed to know it well. When they stopped by a pond Lindy slid off and sat down on a hillock of long grass. Karl stayed on the bike, head bent.

She looked over at him, at the shaggy mop of hair covering his face, the T-shirt riding up his back. She could almost count his vertebrae he was so thin.

Will he speak again? Or was it just the shock, seeing me all covered in blood? She felt her face go hot at the memory. *Maybe he can only do twenty words at a time and by the twenty-first word his throat closes up like mussel shells on the beach or...*

"When I was twelve..." Karl suddenly said, and she jerked up at the sound of his voice. She recognised it from earlier. It was sort of soft and quite deep.

And he's posh. So, not like me then.

"When I was twelve, Dad won the Lottery. Three million pounds."

"You're joking." Lindy couldn't even imagine that much money.

Karl looked round at her. But he didn't carry on speaking. Instead he started to fiddle about with the bike, revving up the engine until she couldn't stand it any longer and yelled, "Switch if off, you muppet!"

The engine cut out. The quiet felt almost too much. She didn't dare say anything out loud in case he took off and drove away.

Then Karl said, "We lived in Portsmouth. I was at the grammar school."

"So you're not a retard?"

Karl stared at her blankly.

"Sorry."

"Dad gave up work. Got a sports car." Karl put his hand to his jaw just below his left ear and massaged it as if it hurt him to speak.

"Mum and Dad wanted to travel," Karl said and he coughed to clear his throat. His voice became more husky as if he had a bad cold. "Not a holiday." More coughs, and when he spoke again his voice sounded strained. "We went away for years."

"Sounds all right to me."

"I want to go to university," Karl said softly, coughing again. His voice settled a bit and he went on. "But we were never in one place long enough to go to school. Anyway, I didn't speak Twi."

"You what?"

"It's from Ghana."

"Where's that?"

"Exactly," said Karl, and he got of the bike and wandered over the grass. She couldn't help thinking he looked a bit like a sulky child. *His parents are rich and they took him abroad. So why stop speaking?*

"They never listened to me," he went on, staring back towards the bike as if wanting to be certain he could make a quick getaway. "I hated travelling. The food, the insects, the stink, always so hot. They said it was good for me. They thought they were giving me 'amazing experiences'."

Karl stopped and his eyebrows furrowed into a deep frown. "But I just wanted to go back to the grammar school with all my friends."

"What's any of this got to do with stopping talking?"

Karl hesitated and his face looked very pale as if he felt sick. Then he walked over to the bike and got back on.

Why bother to tell a saddo like me? The thought of how pathetic she must seem made tears billow in her eyes.

But then Karl settled back on the leather bike seat and, gripping the handlebars, he said, "After a year we went to Turkey. I made a friend there, Musa. He was fourteen, a year older than me. He had a big cousin who took us to the beach in his jeep. Musa's cousin was a bit wild." He stopped again and fiddled with the bike.

"Go on," said Lindy softly, hardly daring to breathe.

"We all went out one evening. It was very hot. His cousin was drinking vodka. Musa took a swig and couldn't stop coughing and we were all laughing. Then his cousin started to drive like a lunatic, swerving all over the place. Musa and me screamed at him to stop and let us out, but he just laughed and then…" Karl's voice dropped to a whisper. "We hit a tree."

Karl fell silent and Lindy realised she was staring at him with her mouth open. She lowered her head.

"I was in the back, got a thump on the head. Musa went through the windscreen." Karl stopped and looked like he was about to break. Then he recovered and said blankly, "Blood ran out of his eyes."

Karl looked over at Lindy, eyes wide with fear. "Musa died," he whispered. "Then afterwards his brothers cut his cousin's throat and he was dead too."

A gull flew overhead, screeching its mocking cry.

"What did your mum and dad say?" said Lindy in a low voice.

"Not much."

Karl tucked his head into his knees and began rocking to and fro.

His parents are well-minted and they're no better than mine are. Musa dead, Jemma dead, Karl silent, Garth in prison. All parents are rubbish.

"Mum and Dad didn't want anything to spoil their hippie dream."

Karl's face was wet with tears. He brushed them away as he went on, "I tried to tell them. I kept saying, 'Musa's dead,' but they always had their maps out, hardly looked up. They didn't listen to me, not even once, they didn't care about Musa. I tried to tell them how bad I felt. I tried."

Karl clenched his fingers together, making a loud cracking sound. "They had their plans and they thought I would get over it, forget about it, move on to the next country. But I couldn't forget and in the end I stopped talking. I suppose there didn't seem any point any more."

A breeze came up and ruffled Karl's hair as Lindy stared down at her feet. The long grass tickled her legs as she tried to picture Karl laughing and talking with his friends in the grammar school. Jess had said he was gifted. *Not much use being gifted if you stop speaking. Jemma was clever, wasn't she? I was going to make sure she didn't go to a rubbish school. But maybe it takes more. Look what's happened to Karl with all his brains.*

"So why did you speak today?" Lindy's mouth felt dry and she licked her lips.

"You know why, Lindy." Karl's eyebrows dipped into a deep concentrated v.

Because of me, he started to speak because he cares about me. A glow settled in the pit of her stomach.

"Why didn't you speak before today, like, in school?"

"Got used to it," said Karl slowly, "It felt like..." he dragged a hand over his eyes, "...like I couldn't actually speak any more. I feel sick most of the time in school. It's horrible. Everyone calls me 'the kid who doesn't speak'. I feel so stupid."

Lindy looked away, embarrassed. *I've been so mean to him, calling him a retard.*

"How long since you spoke?" she said.

Karl stared at her for a long minute and she wondered if perhaps he had forgotten how to speak again. Then he said, "Two years."

"What? No way!" *How can anyone stop speaking for two years?*

"Drove my parents mad. In the end we came back to England to see the doctors."

"They weren't much use then," Lindy snorted.

Karl didn't say anything.

Is he going to tell his parents he can speak again?

"You really didn't speak to anyone, ever?"

He shook his head and then he said, "Just to Jimmy."

"Who's Jimmy?"

"My friend. He's deaf. We use sign language."

Lindy gave a short laugh. "That's not talking! And the housebreaking?"

"It is talking. Anyway, didn't get me anywhere being good." He pointed to the slogan on his T-shirt, 'The Rules Don't Apply to Me'.

Now she understood.

What was the use of talking? No one listens to me either, not Dad, Mum, Garth, none of the teachers. Not Colin, that's for sure. Or Liam. He's not even around any more. He doesn't care about me.

It was very quiet for a moment; not even a gull screamed above them. Lindy looked up at Karl sitting on his bike and a thought came to her. "You're a spiritual refugee," she said.

"What?"

"Like Hamlet. No one listened to Hamlet and no one listens to you at home. Just like me."

Karl stared at her for a long minute and then he nodded and said, "Yes, like you."

Lindy lowered her head again and then she looked at her watch. It was after four. She had to go back to the greenhouse and look after the drugs and wait for Colin.

If I'm not there when he arrives, God knows what he'll do!
The bathroom needed cleaning up too, after all that blood.
What would Karl say if he knew what she was really up to?
He didn't seem to care about the cannabis plants, but what
about cocaine?

She let out a sigh, stood up and brushed her skirt
down. Karl didn't move. She wandered off to the pond,
picked up a stone and threw it angrily across the water.
It curved and fell with an unspectacular plop. When Liam
skimmed stones they bounced up to four times.

So where is he, Lindy? Where's your traveller boyfriend?
It was almost as if Jess was sneering at her.

She turned on her heel and walked back to Karl. "I've got
to go, meeting my cousin Colin at the house. He gets angry
if I'm late."

Karl stared at her for a few seconds and then he walked
over and put his arms around her. Startled, she just stood
there for a minute. Then she let her head rest on his shoulder,
breathing in his light clean smell. It felt different to when
she clung to him on the bike. He began to stroke her hair
very gently, hesitantly, as if he was scared she would snap at
him. *Like I usually do.*

Is he going to kiss me?

Will I let him?

But Karl said, "I'll give you a lift and then wait for you at
the top of the lane. OK?"

She nodded, her head still buried in his shoulder,
her lips suddenly longing for his.

Chapter 16
Night

Karl dropped her at the top of the lane and she walked down, hoping that Colin wouldn't be too long and that Elf hadn't decided to return. Inside, the house felt sticky and hot again, the smell of the plants almost choking her. All the lamps were blazing away and the plants sat smugly in their pots.

"As if butter wouldn't melt in their mouths," Dad would have said.

She stood at the bottom of the stairs for a long minute, not wanting to go back up to the bathroom and see the packets of cocaine again. When she did go up she was shocked at the sight of all the blood on the floor. It had dried into large brown stains. It took ages to scrub it all off and then she kept finding little rusty brown spots. Eagle-eyed, fanatical Colin would spot them all, wouldn't he?

As she was cleaning a particularly stubborn patch she realised that there were other traces of herself she had left all over the house.

Fingerprints! Oh my God!

Even if she did manage to grab Colin's money and escape, she'd be on the run for the rest of her life. If the police came to the greenhouse they would find her fingerprints, strands of her hair, probably even traces of her blood now. She was everywhere; like great huge signposts saying, 'Lindy Bellows was here'.

Then she had another awful thought. *If my fingerprints are here, then so are Karl's.* She was on her knees scrubbing hard at the floor and she looked up at the window where Karl had broken into the house. *His fingerprints are all over the glass.*

Throwing herself to her feet, she ran over to the window and started to rub it hard. But all the while her mind was trawling every corner of the house, thinking of all the places the police could dust for fingerprints. *Mine, Colin's, Elf's and Karl's.*

She felt sick at the thought. She stopped cleaning the window and glanced down at the toilet. There on the seat was the holdall for the packets of cocaine. She had to pack them all away and give the bag to Colin when he arrived. They could have easily done it themselves, but they were making her do it. Colin and Elf were making sure, with everything they made her do, that she was totally part of their so-called 'business'.

It was a long, miserable wait for Colin. She packed the holdall with all the plastic packets and hauled it downstairs. Then she swept the floor and watered the plants. After that, she went all round the house wiping everywhere she thought there might be fingerprints. She knew it was hopeless; there would be more tomorrow and the next day. The hours ticked by and it was nearly eleven before

Colin appeared. She was relieved to see he was alone.

"Saw Elf did you?"

She nodded.

"Did he give you the stuff?"

Lindy handed him the holdall.

"That's my girl. See what I mean, Linds. Family. You can always rely on family." Colin opened the bag and checked the contents. "Nearly done for tonight, just one more little job."

No way, I can't, I mustn't.

"Sean worries if I'm out late."

"You can give him a cut, then." Colin was striding towards the door.

Lindy didn't follow, but kept pushing the broom under the tables.

"Come on then, get a move on."

She only had one more card left to play. "Garth said nothing about any cocaine dealing. I just work in the house with the plants. Garth said you were supposed to help me, he said—"

But Colin grabbed her arm, right on the new wound and she screamed out in pain. He slapped a hand over her mouth, his face so close she could smell the tobacco on his breath. The pain in her arm was so bad she thought she would faint and her knees began to buckle. Colin wrenched her upright, twisting her arm viciously. His eyes were like two mean slits boring into her head. Then he let go, thrusting her backwards. She bent over, massaging her arm, sobbing. A dark patch appeared on her sleeve where the wound had begun to ooze, making her feel faint.

"So it's all right then, Linds? OK?"

She looked up into his face. He was smiling at her as if nothing had happened.

He's insane. Next time he'll kill me and then walk off laughing. How did Garth not see this?

"Get in the car, and we'll be off."

Wiping her eyes dry with the back of her hand, Lindy stumbled behind Colin, feeling like an obedient dog, trained by its master. As they walked to the car, she almost hoped Bag Lady would appear and say something weird to Colin, make him feel he was being watched. But there was no one in the lane and they drove off down the Island, Colin talking all the way.

"It's not much Linds, just a quick delivery and I've got the money, like I said. Here." He held out a wad of notes.

She continued to stare straight ahead, too scared to move.

"Count it."

Slowly she reached out and took the money. Quickly leafing through she nodded and said quietly, "Two hundred." She tucked the roll of notes into the waistband of her school skirt.

"Yeah, that's right; I always pay you, don't I? All I ask for is some family loyalty," and, flicking open a pack of cigarettes with one hand, he offered her one.

She shook her head. *You don't get everything your own way.*

She rested her bad arm on her lap as they drove away. It still hurt a lot and she was worried the wound had opened up. She couldn't go and get it stitched; they'd ask too many questions, wouldn't they? She couldn't believe how cruel Colin had been. He hadn't let go, even when she'd screamed out.

Just like Terrence. And what about Karl? When will Karl turn on me? Everyone else has.

The thought made her feel so mean towards Karl. She eased her arm into a more comfortable position and thought back to the moment when all she wanted was for Karl to kiss her. Did this mean she was no longer faithful to Liam, no longer waiting for him? If she was honest, Liam wasn't real any more; he'd got what he wanted from her and then he'd disappeared. But if Liam could do that to her, then so could Karl. She had to be sure; she wasn't going to be taken in a second time.

Do I have mug written on my forehead? First Liam and then Colin, even Garth's having a laugh at me, setting me up with the job from hell. If Karl's not for real, I'll be ready.

"Here," Colin handed her a comb. He had pulled the car up outside a house near the sea. It was nearly midnight and the Island roads had been so dark and empty, making her feel even more alone. She could see there was a party going on in the house. The front door stood open, music blaring out onto the street. "Make yourself tidy," Colin was telling her. "Tie your hair back, makes you look all sweet and innocent."

"Couldn't I just wait here for you?" *Why can't he go in himself?*

"Too many people know me round here. You're my cover, babes. And don't forget, I'm making it worth your while."

There was nothing she could do, so she tugged the comb through her hair and pulled it back into an elastic band Colin handed her. She could feel tears gathering in her eyes but she couldn't let him see. She knew what would happen if she didn't do what he wanted – he'd made it quite clear, and he didn't care what Garth thought, did he? And anyway, Garth was in prison, well out of the way.

Her arm still throbbed uncomfortably and her head ached from all the questions crowding in. If only she could see Garth for a few minutes and ask him about all this stuff. The prison visit seemed a lifetime away. *If the police catch me, I'll never see Garth again.*

"Here's the gear. Go in and ask for Barry. He'll give you an envelope with the cash."

She took the packet Colin handed her and opened the car door. Suddenly his hand was pressing her shoulder down. "Don't mess up, little cuz," he murmured in her ear and then he tugged a stray lock of her hair back as if he was caressing her. His touch made her shudder and she lurched out of the car and down the path.

Get it over quick as possible and get away. If the police come, I'll have to pretend I was meeting some friends here from school. I'll just drop the packet if there's any sign of trouble.

One thing was certain; if she was caught, Colin would drive off and no one would realise he was the proper dealer.

Inside the house, the party was in full swing, young people in their twenties swigging coloured drinks and dancing to the music. But there were so many people she couldn't get anyone's attention and she began to panic. *I won't find Barry and then Colin will kill me.*

She grabbed a girl's arm but the girl just shook her off and carried on dancing. Then she saw a man standing in a doorway, looking at the crowded room and drinking from a beer bottle. She went over.

"Do you know Barry?" she yelled above the music.

The man stared at her and tipped up his drink, but he gave a curt nod behind him. Lindy saw a man with a shaved head, in a leather jacket and jeans, unscrewing a bottle of spirits in the kitchen. He was on his own. She went up to him.

"Barry?" she said, as quietly as possible.

"Who wants to know?" The man didn't look at her.

"Colin sent me, with, you know, some stuff."

The man turned to gaze at her, looking her up and down, and then he gave a broad grin.

"A schoolgirl. Nice one, Col! Where's the gear?"

She handed him the packet and he pulled an envelope out of his jeans pocket and stuffed it in her hand, his fingers lingering on hers, making her shudder. "Stay and enjoy the party if you want. Lots of guys here like a schoolgirl."

Dirty old man. As if I'd let a bunch of druggies touch me.

She pulled her hand away and turned back to the main room. An old song was pumping out at full blast, one that Garth and Terrence used to play sometimes at home, falling about laughing when they were high on skunk.

It felt as if the whole room was swaying in a drugged stupor and Lindy felt like swaying too. It was so late and she was exhausted. In one corner she saw a girl had collapsed on the floor. Her hair was draped in a pool of spilt beer and her skirt was up round her waist, her knickers showing. No one was taking any notice of her.

She could be dying of an overdose. She might need a paramedic. Someone like me. But instead of going to my St John's Ambulance class tonight, here I am in this filthy room, filled with drunks and druggies.

Lindy was suddenly overwhelmed with hopelessness. What had happened to the future she had planned, away from her stupid family? Becoming a paramedic and proving to all the world that she was different, not like all the other Bellows? As she pushed her way through the steaming crowd, trying not to breathe the air thick with dark clouds of smoke, Lindy felt as though she was being dragged down into some sort of underworld. *Is this my future? Is this all there is for me, drug dealing and mixing with losers like this?*

She thought of Karl, his clean smell, his thin waist and warm body as she snuggled up to him on the bike, his gentle voice when he chose to speak and his wonderful eyebrows saying more than words ever could. Karl wasn't like this; Karl was different. Couldn't she be different too?

She was almost blind with tears as she pushed her way out of the house and back to the car. She managed to wipe her tears away before Colin spotted she had been crying.

"Got it?" Colin's hand stretched out towards her, his eyes bright with greed. He grabbed the envelope and stuffed it into his inside pocket. Then he turned the ignition key and they screeched away. Lindy fell back, banging her wounded arm again on the dashboard.

He doesn't care what happens to me, so long as he gets his money.

Colin crowed all the way back to the greenhouse. "You done good, Lindy, like I always said you would. I'd take you home, babes, but I gotta meet Elf. You call a taxi, eh? Here's the number and an extra twenty quid for expenses. You just remember you're the one that I want. You're part of the business now, cuz."

His words ground a hole in her stomach. She wanted to unlock the car door and throw herself onto the tarmac. So what if she was killed? No one would miss another Bellows. Who would care?

Colin stopped the car on the main road, at the top of the lane and, with a cheery wave, drove off. It was very dark and the street lights seemed to be out on this bit of the road. The wind was blowing hard, bending the tall pines towards her menacingly. Looking over her shoulder all the way,

Lindy half-ran, half-walked towards the bridge. *Where can I get a taxi round here? I don't even know if the bus runs this late. I can't walk all the way back home in the dark.* Night sounds were all around, the ghostly hooting of an owl and the high-pitched bark of a dog or maybe a fox. *Do foxes attack like wolves?*

She could see Langstone Bridge lit up in the distance and looked about for Karl, but no, of course he wouldn't still be waiting for her. She'd been hours and hours.

It was too late for a bus. She would have to walk. Hugging her arms around her chest, tears beginning to gather in her eyes again, she set off along the empty road. Every sound made her jump and her mind was a whirl of crazy thoughts; ghosts and vampires, wolves and unnamed monsters. The world was a dangerous place and she was all alone. Hot tears spilled down her cheeks.

Then she heard the familiar sound of a motorbike engine. Whipping round, she saw Karl drive up. He stopped in front of her. Silently she climbed on and, putting her arms round his waist, she rested her head on his back and let her mind go blank as Karl turned the bike around and drove off.

Chapter 17
Beach Bum

They cruised all the way down the Island, past the funfair with its coloured lights gleaming enticingly, and onto the road towards the ferry. Karl carried on past the lake where he had stopped earlier and told Lindy about his silence and Musa. The road wound on and on until they reached a small bay with chalets at the far end. Karl stopped the bike beside a houseboat drawn up on the beach. In the quiet after the roar of the engine, Lindy could hear waves pulling gently across the pebbles on the beach. The scent in the air was a mixture of salt and pine. They jumped off the bike and Karl pulled it onto its stand.

"What are we doing here?" said Lindy.

Karl said nothing and went up a short flight of steps to the door. He tried it, but it was locked, so he took out his penknife and started to fiddle with the lock. Within seconds it had released and he pushed open the door.

Lindy hesitated. *He can break in anywhere, can't he? What if there's someone in there?*

But the houseboat was empty. Karl found a candle and some matches and the flame lit up the small space. There was an old sofa, a small table and chairs and a tiny sink with a camping stove next to it. The boat smelt musty and neglected.

134

"Let's go for a swim," said Karl.

"You're crazy, it's dark."

"Full moon," said Karl, already pulling off his sweatshirt.

"It's freezing!"

"Be warmer in the water." His eyes caught hers and for a moment they stared unblinking at each other.

"I haven't got my bikini with me." *Can't even swim.*

"What're you wearing underneath?" said Karl and he slipped off his jeans revealing a pair of black boxer shorts.

Lindy tried to remember what pants she was wearing. *Girl boxers, shoplifted last year.* They almost looked like shorts and she always wore a T-shirt under her uniform. Suddenly she was longing to slip off her blood-stained clothes and immerse herself in the sea, wash clean the mess of the day. Then she remembered her arm.

"What about the dressings?"

"Just go in up to your waist."

Karl's eyebrows were knitted so appealingly she couldn't resist. She hesitated for a moment, looking at his slight, bare chest in the candlelight and then she stripped off her uniform and kicked it into a corner.

They ran out the door and onto the beach. Karl raced into the water like a happy dog. Within seconds he was striking out in a powerful crawl. Lindy tested the water with her toes and it wasn't as cold as she had imagined. She waded in, keeping her left arm high. The moon lit up the water straight head of her in a great swathe of white. As she waved her right hand across the surface of the water, she was startled to see it light up a fluorescent green. It was so beautiful! The moon, the green shining water... she forgot about the cold and waded to and fro. Karl rose and fell ahead of her like a dolphin playing in the water.

Then he was standing in front of her, bare to his waist, water dripping from his floppy hair. "Its phosphorescence," he said smiling.

"Looks like diamond sprinkles."

Karl waved his hand over the shimmering water. "They're crustaceans."

"You what?"

"Like really tiny lobsters. They come in on the tide. It's quite rare."

He was standing very close and she could smell his skin, so clean and pure. He reached out and looped a stray lock of her hair behind her ear. She thought he would kiss her and she decided to let him. But then he lowered his eyes and ducked away, wading back through the shallows, his thin shoulders gleaming a ghostly white in the moonlight.

When they got back to the boat Lindy started to shiver. Karl rummaged around and found a towel. There was a man's shirt and a pair of jeans hanging over the back of a chair and he handed them to Lindy.

"Want to have a fire on the beach?" said Karl and he still sounded like someone trying out speech for the first time, his sentences clipped, his choice of words simple.

"Be with you in a moment."

Once he'd gone Lindy searched her stained uniform until she found Colin's money lying in a crumpled heap on the floor. For a moment she was tempted to take it outside and toss it on the fire. *That's what Karl would do, he burnt the fifty pound note to show me what he thought of Colin and his cannabis house. I should do the same.* She picked the money up and started towards the door but then she stopped. *I need all the money I can get if I'm ever going to get away from Colin and Elf.*

Lindy stuffed the notes into the pocket of the jeans, glancing up nervously to make sure Karl didn't see. He might think she'd stolen it and she didn't want that. *That's not me, I'm different. Whatever Colin, Elf and my rubbish family think. Karl knows, I'm sure he does.*

Picking up her blood-stained uniform, she went outside. She had to get rid of her clothes; she couldn't stand the sight of the blood any longer. *Anyway, if I'm planning to run away, I'm finished with school.* But she felt very empty inside to think that she wouldn't go back to English and see what happened to Hamlet.

Mr Davies had once told her to try harder, "You could get a good grade if you put your mind to it, Lindy Bellows." There were sniggers round the class and Lindy had just shrugged, but inside she had felt quite pleased.

Joyce in the Ambulance said that she needed her exams to train to be a paramedic. "But that's no problem for a bright girl like you, Lindy, is it?"

So Joyce thought she was clever, maybe even Mr Davies

did too; but Colin thought she was only fit to be a drug dealer. *What does Karl think?*

Karl had started a fire on the beach, it was only small but it was burning well. He didn't say anything as she threw her clothes into the middle but poked the fire with a stick to make sure the flames licked up over the stained uniform. They stood there for a while, watching the fire, the sound of waves dragging back and forward over the beach.

Karl went to get more driftwood and came back with an armful. After he had built up the fire, they sat quietly for a long time. Lindy was beginning to wonder if he had forgotten how to speak again. Perhaps he could only do short bursts after all this time. Part of her wished they could stay like this for ever. It made her feel so calm, as though her worries had all dropped away, sitting here in silence with Karl. Karl's world had its attractions.

But then Karl suddenly said, "I thought I'd just get over it."

"Not talking?"

He nodded. "I wanted to be the same as everyone else. You don't feel normal if people talk to you and you don't talk back. They think you're weird, or stupid or..." He stopped and threw a few twigs on the fire. "The longer you don't speak, the harder it is to start again. It's like a trap."

Like me in Colin's trap. The longer I stay, the more trapped I am.

Then Karl said, "My voice sounds funny. I thought everyone would laugh at me if I started talking."

"You have a nice voice," said Lindy quietly.

"I do?"

She nodded.

Karl stood up and rummaged around further up the beach for more sticks. When he came back she looked up at him and said, "So, do you think you'll go on talking now you've started?"

He looked down at her, his eyes serious, his eyebrows levelled in a thick dark line, and then he said, "Yes, I think so."

After that there didn't seem to be anything else to say and they sat watching the fire creep along the driftwood, holding out their hands to the warmth, until Karl said, "I read it in a book."

"What?"

"How to take a window out. I scraped off the putty with my knife. That's what I most like doing."

"Housebreaking?"

"Reading. I love facts."

"What kind of facts?" They didn't have any books in her house. She and Mum read magazines. But she had liked reading *Hamlet* in class, hadn't she? And it had been nice reading stories to Jemma. She remembered one book about a boy whose mother ignored him so much he was eaten by a monster, who then took the boy's place at home, but his mother still didn't notice. *Just like our house.*

Karl suddenly said, "Britain is the eighth largest island in the world; Italy won the world cup in 1934, 1938, 1982 and

2006; Hayling Island has a population of 18,250; the *Titanic* was launched from Belfast dockyard on May 31st 1911..." Karl went on and on until she thought he would never stop. She had never heard so many facts in one go. Then his voice gave out, hoarse with the effort of such a long speech.

Lindy bent down and poked at the fire with a bit of bleached driftwood for a while, her mind confused. *So he's not dumb. I was right the first time; he's a genius. All those times I called him a retard...* to cover her embarrassment she turned to Karl and declared expansively, "You're clever, really clever, a boffin."

Karl shrugged and his head dipped down to his drawn-up knees. "Doesn't matter."

"What?"

"No one notices."

"Who, Mummy and Daddy?" said Lindy in a teasing voice, and Karl flinched. "Who cares? They sound just like mine, losers."

"Need them, don't you?"

"You're not twelve any more Karl. When are you sixteen?"

"November."

"Older than me, I'm not sixteen until January. You don't need no one. You decide what you want, not your parents." Lindy picked up a stone and threw it into the fire, sending a shower of sparks into the dark sky.

"We're spiritual refugees, you and me, just like Hamlet. You know what he said?"

Karl shook his head.

"'The time is out of joint.'"

"Meaning?"

"Everything's wrong, sick, messed up."

Lindy stopped for a minute but Karl didn't speak. This felt different, telling Karl what to do, leading the way.

She went on in a stronger voice, "So we have to put it right. No one else is going to do it for us. Hamlet knew that, too."

Karl stared up at her and said quietly, "Who's the boffin now?"

Lindy ducked her head to hide how pleased she felt.

The moon slid behind a new bank of clouds and the first drops of heavy rain began to fall.

They damped down the fire with sand and ran back into the houseboat. The sound of rain on the wooden roof thundered like the rolling of drums. Lindy rifled around in a cupboard, looking for something to eat.

Then Karl said, "We could sleep here tonight!"

"I'm not sleeping with you!"

"No, I didn't mean... Never mind, we'll go back."

Lindy sat down on one of the upright chairs. She was tired and cold, and didn't really want to ride all the way back home in the pouring rain. She looked at the sofa; it pulled out into a double bed. "I suppose we could. But we're putting a cushion down the middle."

"Course. Like a sleepover. No one will come here this time of night."

Karl pulled out the sofa, arranged a military line of

cushions down the centre and found a couple of blankets in a drawer. "There we go – shipshape and ready to sail," he said, grinning slightly in the flickering light.

Lindy couldn't help grinning back, he looked so cute.

She lay down on the side nearest the wall and closed her eyes. She could hear small sounds of Karl getting ready for bed, tidying up their shoes and making sure the door was locked.

She had only spent one night with Liam, in his uncle's trailer. It was a frosty night but nothing would persuade Liam to close the window. "Like being in prison again," he had said. He had told her all about being locked up when he was seventeen for stealing cars. "No air in prison, just stink."

What would it feel like with Karl? Does he want to do it? Do I?

"All right?" said Karl.

She opened one eye.

"Shall I blow out the candle?"

She nodded.

Darkness fell over the room. Lindy felt the mattress shift as he lay down and she could smell the salt in his hair. *He probably swims a lot. That's what a lonely person who doesn't speak would do. Did he really never ever speak, since Musa died?*

"You must have spoken sometimes?" she whispered.

Karl didn't answer and she thought he had fallen asleep in the enveloping dark of the houseboat.

Then he whispered back, "No."

"What if you needed something, like, I dunno, like a pee?"

They burst into giggles.

"I mean, what if you're in some foreign country and you don't know where the bogs are?"

"Follow the smell."

They both burst out laughing again, then gradually fell silent. Lindy could feel her body relaxing to the rhythm of Karl's breathing.

Then Karl whispered, "You asleep?"

The sound of a boat engine chugged away in the distance. She whispered back, "No, are you?"

Another pause and then Karl said, "Promise me something?"

"What?"

"You won't ever cut yourself again."

She didn't trust herself to speak.

"Promise, Lindy," he said again, and this time his voice was almost fierce.

She felt his breath on her face, he was very close now and she didn't know what she wanted. So she just said, "OK."

After that the silence between them deepened and Lindy finally drifted off, entering the tunnel that had been beckoning all day. But this time she wasn't frightened and strode along until she came to the bottom of a steep staircase flooded with white light. By now her legs were weighed down with clumps of seaweed and pebbles caught between her toes.

Must have been from the swim; me, Karl and the dolphins, swimming in the deep blue sea.

But she had to climb the staircase because Karl had said there was a great prize at the top. And what if it was three million pounds? So she dragged her heavy legs painfully up each of the thirty-three steps. But there wasn't any money. Instead, on the top step, with fluffy red hair, a halo of bright light gleaming around her, sat baby Jemma. "Linloo," she cooed, "Linloo." Lindy stretched out her arms.

Then she woke up.

Sunlight was streaming through the open door and there was the smell of bacon frying. Karl was standing by the camping stove, laying rashers into a pan.

"Where did you get that?" she asked, still wrapped up in the dream.

"Shop. Been up for hours. Let's skip school today."

Chapter 18
Ammunition

It was past midday when they finally drove back to Lindy's house. She was seeing Garth at the prison at three with Mum and they had to get the bus. When they arrived at her front gate, Lindy slipped down from the pillion and said, "Bye then. See you in school tomorrow."

But as she put her key in the lock, Karl was right behind her. *No way, he's not coming into this dump.*

She turned and his face was so close to hers that their lips almost brushed. She gave him a little push and said, "Off you go."

"But I thought I could..."

"I said, no. End of."

Lindy stepped into the hallway, but before she could shut the door in Karl's face, Sean called out from the living room, "Lindy! I've been waiting and waiting."

She slipped into the living room, Karl close on her heels and pushed the door shut.

"What's up?" said Lindy, her heart sinking that Sean was not in school. Now Karl would see what a rubbish family she came from.

Sean looked as if he had slept in his clothes. There were dark rings under his eyes and his face was grubby.

"You didn't come home last night," he said. He was clutching a plastic bag to his chest, something heavy inside.

Lindy could hear Karl breathing lightly behind her and in the kitchen Mum was running water in the sink.

Sean began to wheeze but he didn't get his inhaler out. "I came looking for you." Lindy pulled Sean's inhaler out of his pocket and handed it to him. Sean turned away and, shaking the inhaler vigorously, took two rapid puffs. His breathing settled down and he turned back again.

"You nicked something?" asked Lindy, pointing at the bag.

"I know where you've been, I followed you on Darren's bike," said Sean.

Lindy could almost feel Karl's heart rate double as she met his gaze. His eyebrows arched up, but he said nothing.

"What do you mean?"

Before Sean could reply there was a creaking sound and the door opened slowly. Mum appeared, dressing gown open to reveal a grubby nightdress. "Got your friend in, girl?" she said. "Well, make him a cup of tea, we can all watch TV, sure enough." She slumped down in an armchair, raising the volume on the remote control.

Lindy shook her head in disbelief and muttered, "We're going to my room."

She turned abruptly, pushing Sean ahead of her upstairs, not daring to think of the mess she had left the room in the day before.

She managed to pull the bathroom door shut on the way, closing in the stink, but the bedroom looked like a car crash. Clothes, bedding, old crisp packets and bits of first-aid stuff were thrown everywhere.

Karl didn't seem bothered. He sat down on the edge of Sean's bed and looked at the cot. "Where's the baby?"

"She's dead," said Lindy, and a cold silence filled the room.

The silence lasted so long that Lindy was sure Karl was inventing an excuse to leave.

But then he said, "Yours, or...?"

"My baby sister."

"Sorry. I mean... sorry." Karl ducked his head and his hair flopped over his face.

Lindy started to straighten the bed and then gave up; it was too late to tidy up.

"What happened?" asked Karl.

Sean was fiddling with some toy cars on the windowsill.

"Meningitis," said Lindy. "She died in her sleep; nothing we could do was there, Sean?"

Sean turned round, his eyes sunk into his thin face, the bones of his skull sharper than ever through his pale skin. "You didn't come home last night and I was scared, so I followed you. I've followed you lots of times." His voice echoed thin and shrill in the bedroom.

Lindy was too shocked to speak. What had he seen? What did he know?

"When I went back this morning," Sean carried on,

"I saw the whitey man in the suit."

Elf. Lindy felt a knife of fear go through her.

"I was scared, Lindy. What if something happened? What if you died, like—"

"Don't be mental."

They both stared at the cot. Then Sean went on, "I saw the whitey man go in the house. His big car was parked outside so I looked in the car. There was something pink on the floor; I thought it was your best top. He might've beat you up, or killed you. I tried the car door, like Terrence showed me..."

"You what?"

"You know, when we went round the streets, we found lots of cars that were never locked."

Lindy groaned but Sean carried on. "The door opened but the pink thing was just an old shirt. I found the bag under the seat and I was just going to look but then a dog bit me." He pulled up his jeans to show a sore patch with tiny teeth marks showing clearly in his pale skin. "And so I ran but I was still holding this." He gestured at the bag.

Lindy leaned against the door of the wardrobe and closed her eyes.

"The lady said the dog's name is Prince something. It don't hurt much."

This was a nightmare. *Sean and Elf in the same place. Sean getting into Elf's car and stealing something.* Lindy didn't even want to look in the bag. *What if it's drugs?*

And why was Bag Lady and her stupid dog nosing round outside the greenhouse? How soon before she calls the police or Colin finds out?

Colin will kill me. No, that's Elf's job!

"What's in the bag?" asked Karl.

Sean stared at him for a second and then reached in and pulled out a brown padded envelope. He let the bag drop and, putting his hand into the neck of the envelope, drew out a silver handgun, its weight pulling his hand down.

"This," said Sean raising the gun to his eye and squinting along the barrel.

"Give it here, you idiot!" snapped Karl. Sean was so startled that he almost dropped the gun. Karl grabbed it and clumsily levered out a clip of bullets.

"I could sell it for a ton," said Sean.

Karl ignored him and said to Lindy, "I'll get rid of this."

"No, it's not your problem," Lindy protested, but Karl was already halfway down the stairs.

Lindy was just about to follow him when her mum appeared at the bedroom door. She was dressed in a faded purple track suit, straggly hair dragged back in an elastic band, handbag clutched in her left hand.

Lindy heard the front door close. Karl was gone.

"You ready, girl?"

"What?"

"Going to see Garth, sure enough, and isn't the ten past bus due now?"

As they walked to the bus stop, Lindy felt as though

carpet tape was being wound slowly round and round her head and body, tighter and tighter. She was trapped like a fly in a spider's web and it was Colin who would order Elf to slowly rip off her wings.

Chapter 19
Inside

How could Sean be so stupid? It's bad enough he followed me to the greenhouse, but stealing Elf's gun... And now Karl's involved. I've turned sweet little Karl into a criminal.

Sean's words before he ran out of the bedroom rolled round and round inside her head all the way to the prison gates.

"I'll go after Karl," Sean had said, "make sure he's OK, with, you know..."

He was out of the front door before Lindy could stop him and anyway, what could she do? Her mother was pulling at her arm, worried about missing the bus and she had to see Garth – she couldn't cope with Colin any longer. But leaving Sean to run around like a loose cannon seemed like the worst end of a horror film. There was no telling what he might do next.

What if Sean goes back to Colin's house and Bag Lady is in the lane and he tells her about Karl and the gun. She'll telephone the police and the police will race out after Karl on his motorbike, it's not that powerful, it can't outrun a police car, with all the sirens and everything. And Karl will be arrested for handling firearms, Sean will be arrested and put in prison with insane Terrence and they probably make

151

brothers share cells and Karl might even skid and end up dead like Musa in Turkey. Then he'll never ever speak again. It's all my fault. I hate Colin and...

Even thinking about Elf froze her blood. What if he got hold of Sean?

I should have killed myself with Dad's razor.

The bus lumbered into a lay-by and stopped. They had arrived at the prison. There was no more time to think as they followed the straggly crowd of women, some with young children, through the double doors and into the reception area.

"No stamps, cigarettes, money..." the prison officer droned at them as they stood in line to be searched.

"Last time this man had a chocolate bar with him for his son and they made him throw it away, sure enough," her mother muttered to Lindy. "And will you tell me now what harm is a chocolate bar?"

They submitted to the search, and then they were slammed through three sets of gates and up a flight of stairs into a long room. Lindy could see bars on the windows. They made her shudder. The prisoners all wore red sashes like in school teams.

Garth was sitting at the far end. He stood up and nodded awkwardly when they approached. "All right?"

Mum reached up and threw her arms around Garth's neck, clinging tightly as if she would never let go. Eventually he gently pushed her away and sat her down. Lindy saw her wipe a tear away with the corner of her top. Lindy stayed standing until Garth leaned over and gave her a light hug. *How am I going to speak to him about Colin with Mum sitting here?* She hadn't thought of that.

Her mother started talking quickly, as if to hide how upset she was feeling.

"So tell me now, son, how much longer you in here for? Your Da says another twelve months but I said no, surely not, I said only another ten months, isn't it?" She paused and Garth opened his mouth to speak, but she cut in, "Missing you something terrible, that I am."

There was an awkward silence as Mum blew her nose and Lindy stared at the floor. Then Garth said, "Ten months and two weeks."

But his voice sounded distant and Lindy looked up to see him staring hard at her.

"Mum, go and get us all a cup of tea and some of those chocolate bars I like would you?" Garth was still staring at Lindy.

What's his problem?

"You go, Lindy," said her mother, reaching into her handbag for some pound coins.

But Garth said firmly, "No, you go. Please, Mum."

Her mother stood up. She muttered a bit but she went off to join the queue at the other end of the room.

As soon as she was out of hearing Garth leaned forward and said in a low voice, "I don't want you working for Colin no more, OK?"

Lindy stared at him amazed.

"You listening, sis? He's got into something really bad has Colin. Mate of mine in here tipped me off. Col's gone in with a bloke called Elf: very, very dangerous. Elf's into international drug dealing, South American suppliers of cocaine, he's importing tonnes of it through the ports, millions of pounds. And he's bad, sis. Colin's gone too far."

Lindy could hardly believe what she was hearing. Her voice cracked when she spoke up. "You're the one who's gone too far, it's too late! Colin's got me dealing and Elf was in the house last night, sorting out the drugs."

Even Lindy was surprised at the look of sheer horror that came over Garth's face when she mentioned Elf.

"You're already mixed up with Elf! That low-life scum! You've got to get out, Lindy! Now!"

Garth was almost choking with the effort of trying to keep his voice down, so as not to attract the attention of the guards.

"He came to the cannabis house. He's keeping cocaine there. Thousands of pounds worth! And I can't stop working for Colin now! Why did you do this to me, Garth?"

Lindy looked round for her mum. Fortunately there was a long queue and Mum was at the back of it.

Garth dragged a hand across his face, "What's Colin up to letting that maniac near you." His voice broke. "I thought I was doing the right thing, sis. Banged up in here, I couldn't help you no more. I knew how you was after Jemma died and then there's Sean running wild. I asked Col to give you that job, just a bit of gardening for some extra cash. I didn't know anything about cocaine dealing and that scum, Elf. Not 'til my mate told me in here."

"I had to meet Elf all on my own," said Lindy in a low voice. "I was so scared. He had a whole suitcase full of bags of cocaine."

Garth nodded.

"Colin's been planning this all along," Lindy went on. "He drove me round to someone's house and I had to go in, hand over the drugs and collect the cash. He just sat in the car. What if the police catch me?"

"They won't, Lindy, I promise," muttered Garth, leaning towards her.

One of the prison wardens strolled past and Lindy jumped, while Garth straightened up and gave the warden a friendly grin.

Oh my God! What if he hears what we're saying? It's like there are spies everywhere. Why doesn't Garth understand?

"Colin's trapped me, can't you see? He says I'll go to prison if he gets caught, he'll make sure of it," and Lindy swallowed down a painful sob.

Garth's face was flushed with anger. He leaned forward again and said, "OK, sis, calm down. I swear I never knew Colin would mix you up with coke and a psycho like Elf. And I promise I'll deal with them both when I get out."

"But that's too late," hissed Lindy. "Me and Sean've got to get away. Maybe we'll go and live with Liam after all, if I can find him."

"Who? That nonce from the fairground? No, he's no

good. Listen, Mum'll be back in a minute, you gotta listen. I'll get you out of this, I promise. I never meant for all this to happen." Garth leaned forward and spoke in a tight whisper. "This is what you got to do. Get to Colin's boat, *Trojan 3*; he moors it somewhere off Hayling Island. I can't remember the exact spot but there are some rusty boats and a pebble beach. You got to get hold of his computer. He'll have all the deals with Elf on there. If you can get that information to the police..."

"Grass him up?"

"Yeah."

"But he's our cousin!"

Garth fixed her with a hard stare, "You're my sister, Linds, you come before that lunatic. Who can help you find the boat? Someone you can trust?"

Only Karl and maybe after today...

Lindy gave a shrug. The warden walked past them again and seemed to pick them out specially. *He knows. He can hear what we're saying; they'll arrest me before I get to the bus.* But then his attention was caught by a couple rowing in the far corner and he moved away.

"Lindy, are you listening?" Garth was speaking in an urgent whisper. "Get into that computer, find out where they're meeting those dealers from South America and then tip the police off. My mate in here says there's a big deal going down on Thursday. Trust me, sis, they'll put Col and Elf away for ever. But don't let those scumbags know it's you, Lindy. Elf's evil, he'll kill anyone who gets in his way—"

"They didn't have the chocolate I normally get you because of the deliveries." Lindy's mum had returned. "The lady said the road-works were something terrible this morning and the van didn't get here."

Lindy dried her eyes and throughout the rest of the visit she repeated *Trojan 3, Trojan 3* over and over to herself to make sure she wouldn't forget.

When they were leaving, Garth pulled her towards him and, as he hugged her, he whispered in her ear, "It'll be all right, I promise. And that cannabis house? I'm getting a mate on the outside to burn it to the ground, no one will ever know you was there. Trust me, sis."

His big arms encased her like Liam's used to, and she wanted to stay there for ever: safe and protected.

But a warden called out, "Come along, Bellows," and Garth melted away, leaving Lindy with her mother, still grumbling about the chocolate.

Chapter 20
Razor

Lindy stared out of the bus window as they pulled away from the prison. There was so much to do and Garth wouldn't be able to help her much more. How was she going to manage everything by herself?

Then she heard what sounded like a muffled sob and turned to see her mother wiping tears from her eyes.

"Mum?"

"Aye?" Her mum blew her nose on a tissue. Then she said, "It's terrible hard my boys being in prison, girl, and then what with the baby..." Her voice trailed off.

Garth's words ran through her mind, "Every sad thought leads back to Jemma, don't it, sis?" Lindy felt tears well up herself.

"Your Da, he tries sure enough," Mum went on. "But it's terrible hard now, isn't it?" She wiped her eyes again. "What with the house half empty..."

Lindy reached out and gingerly pulled Mum's hand towards her. It felt thin and bony and quite cold. Her mother used to hold her hand to cross roads when she was a little girl. But that was years ago. *Maybe she won't like it now.*

But her mother gripped Lindy's hand back tightly,

as if she had been thrown a lifeline. They stayed like that, not speaking, all the way back to the estate.

As they walked up the front path to the house her mother said, "You can be a good girl, can't you now."

Lindy didn't say anything but she felt a little glow inside as Mum leant towards her, turning the key in the lock.

Once in the house, Lindy said, "I need a bath, any hot water?"

"I put it on this morning, come to think of it. Off you go and have a good soak now. I'll put the kettle on."

Lindy ran upstairs and ran a deep bath. As she lay in the bath, she thought about when she took her mother's hand on the bus. She remembered what Joyce used to say: "A good paramedic needs to be able to show people they care, have sympathy. So develop your bedside manner." Joyce would have been pleased with her, wouldn't she?

But as she was drying herself in the bedroom and rooting around for clean clothes, everything she had to do came crowding back into her mind. It was overwhelming.

I've got to find Sean and keep him away from the lane and from Bag Lady and Elf.

Then she had to find Karl and tell him about Colin's boat. Karl would help her, wouldn't he? But maybe he wouldn't now. After all, he had found his voice again. Imagine, after two years of not talking, to suddenly start up. Like a blind person being able to see. Or a cripple getting up and walking. Karl was clever; he wouldn't want to bother with a saddo like her, would he?

He'd probably already gone back to school, collected his homework and sucked up to all the posh teachers in the top sets.

Lindy stared at her reflection in the mirror on the inside of the wardrobe door. Her face seemed even paler than ever and her hair was damp and straggly. There were large dark circles under her eyes and the wounds on her arm looked like gaping red mouths.

Good thing my Liam can't see me like this.

But it was just habit to think about Liam, now. She hardly felt anything for him any more.

Face it Lindy, Liam's gone for good. But Karl is still here and you need him.

She had to find Sean before he decided to do something completely insane, like break into Colin's house right in front of Bag Lady or someone else in the lane. He was only nine. Then they'd call the police and they'd all be in big trouble. Everyone, of course, except Colin and Elf. They would make sure they got clean away.

Lindy felt the pressure rising inside her and thought briefly of the razor and the relief of cutting herself.

"No, no," she moaned quietly. "No time for that now."

She pulled on an almost-clean T-shirt and a pair of jeans. She still had the two hundred pounds Colin had given her last night, and she stuffed it into her pocket. *Who knows what I'll need today.*

Then she ran downstairs. She could hear the television in the living room announcing the six o'clock news. Her dad was back and she caught the words, "Gotta face it, Colleen, none of them turned out good. The boys banged up, Sean never home and Jemma…" His voice faded away and Lindy turned to go, but then she heard her mum say her name and something about Colin.

"That worthless piece of scum," said Dad.

Dad knew Colin was no good; he tried to warn me. Why didn't I listen?

Lindy slammed the front door and ran to the bus stop. The important thing now was to find Sean.

As she took her seat on the bus to the Island, Lindy felt her fingers close around the money in her jeans pocket. Without thinking she had also picked up the key to the greenhouse.

Suppose I can't stop doing my job yet. I'll find Sean, send him home and then go and water those disgusting plants. Can't make Colin suspicious.

The bus swung over Langstone Bridge. The tide was in and windsurfers and yachters were skimming across the water in the bright evening sunshine. It seemed to Lindy that the whole world had a different life to her; carefree, simple, straightforward. The mess she was in was getting worse and worse and now she was relying on Karl to help her sort it out.

Why did he run off with the gun? Maybe he's not who he says he is, housebreaking and stuff. I trusted him. But then I trusted Colin and look where that got me.

As Lindy got down from the bus at the top of the lane,

she could hear a dog barking in the direction of the greenhouse. She broke into a run, and as she reached the house she could see Sean talking to Bag Lady. Prince William was jumping around at her feet.

"What are you doing here?" Lindy grabbed Sean's arm and pulled him around to face her. This seemed to drive the dog into a greater frenzy and he jumped up at Lindy and nipped her hand. She shook him away and aimed her foot at his underbelly. The dog gave a high-pitched yelp.

"They do that when there's bad air around," Bag Lady said in a shrill voice.

Lindy turned back to her. "What do you want?"

"I want clear air, don't you? The government's always saying they're going to give us clean air. But Prince William knows, don't he? What are you two doing in there?" Bag Lady nodded towards the cannabis house.

Quick as a flash, Sean said. "Gardening for our uncle, innit Lindy?"

Lindy was struck by the irony of this but managed to smile at Sean and nod. "Yeah, that's right. Well go on, get on with it."

Sean opened the garden gate and started pulling up weeds along the path.

"You get a funny smell here sometimes," Bag Lady muttered, "when the wind comes off the fields. Them farmers, growing stuff. It's not all food, you know."

What does she mean? What does she know?

But before Lindy could think of anything to distract

Bag Lady, the little spaniel gave a sharp bark and scampered off up the path to the door of the greenhouse. He began scrabbling about, as if he was trying to squeeze right under the door and into the house. Lindy started to follow but Bag Lady scurried ahead of her, calling, "What you found, what you got there? Proper little scallywag, my Prince William."

Lindy raced up the path and grabbed the old woman's arm.

"Is this a mugging?" Bag Lady inquired, staring up into Lindy's face, her eyes black as a tiny bird's. "Because I've only got five pence in my bag today, dear."

Bag Lady began to poke around at the bottom of the door with her foot, muttering under her breath, and then suddenly she said, "Plants need lots of water, don't they?"

Oh God! Just shut up you old bat. Lindy wracked her brains for an answer and then it was as though a light switched on inside her. *Money!* Garth used to say, "Money always works, sis, everything in life's just business."

She pulled a ten pound note out of her pocket and thrust it at Bag Lady. "Here. Go and buy dog food, teabags, whatever old people like, but just go home. We're busy."

She glanced over her shoulder at Sean, who was on his hands and knees now, looking as if he did gardening every day.

"But what about water for the plants?" asked the old woman.

Lindy looked at her in despair. *She can't get in the house, can she? What has she seen already?*

In a last desperate act she scooped the little dog into her arms and strode off down the path, waving the ten pound note. She was in luck, for once. Bag Lady followed her, ticking off a shopping list on her fingers, "Oh, I need bacon, bread, beans, butter..."

Once out of the gate, Bag Lady grabbed the money, stuffed it in her pocket and then, nodding her head, she walked off down the lane, the little dog running and jumping beside her.

Lindy felt her legs go weak. *Almost caught, almost given away; how much more of this can I take?* For a fleeting moment she imagined breaking into Bag Lady's cottage and tying her up. Just until she had finished with Colin.

Sean broke into her thoughts. "Did I do OK, Lindy?"

She whipped round, wanting to scream at him that he'd nearly ruined everything; but he looked so scared and close to tears, just like a little boy, that she gave a tight laugh and said, "You did fine, OK?"

Sean shrugged and didn't say anything.

"Karl isn't here," she continued in a low voice. "I don't know where he's gone, but he won't come back here with the gun. You have to go home, now." She started to tug him back up the lane towards the road.

"What about you? The whitey man might come back," whined Sean as they reached the main road.

"Got some business to see to. Here's some cash, get the bus home, get fish and chips, whatever, but stay at home until I get back." Lindy glared at Sean so fiercely that he just nodded and walked off to the bus stop.

Lindy let herself into Colin's house and started to fill the watering can.

Now what am I going to do?

Chapter 21
Trojan Horse

It was already evening and the house felt eerily silent. Lindy went upstairs to the front room and peered through a chink in the blackout curtains into the lane. There was no sign of Bag Lady or the dog and she couldn't see Sean sneaking back either. But what about Karl? She didn't like to think what he might be doing right now, with Elf's gun. Maybe Karl was part of a gang, like Terrence's gang. *Joak boyz*, they called themselves. They sprayed it in black and white all over the estate. Karl didn't seem like a gang member, with those cute eyebrows and all his different ways of speaking without using any words. But he seemed to know what to do with the gun. *Maybe he just wants to keep it.*

Who cares what Karl wants. Find Colin's boat, find it and get inside it. Get hold of that computer and quickly.

She could use some of Colin's money to pay someone to help her find *Trojan 3*. But they would wonder why she was going onto someone else's boat and anyhow it would be locked like the houseboat was. Colin would definitely lock his boat up. She couldn't do it on her own.

She was running out of options and she knew where that left her. Karl. She had to find him in school tomorrow and

166

make him help her. Tomorrow she'd find him. Karl could break into anything and he had a credit card. If necessary he could buy a boat to take them into the harbour.

She caught the bus home and let herself into the house. The telly was blaring in the front room and she could smell fish and chips. She turned as she heard a light footstep on the stairs. It was Sean.

"I put yours in the oven to keep warm," he said.

She could see he was trying to be good and she realised that she hadn't eaten since breakfast with Karl. "Come on then. Let's take it upstairs."

Sean grinned and fussed around, opening the oven and taking out the greasy packet. He rinsed a plate in the sink and laid out the food, smothering it with a thick swirl of ketchup, just how Lindy liked it. Then he pulled a can of Coke out of the fridge and followed her upstairs carrying the plate.

They sat opposite each other on their beds and Sean started, "I didn't tell the old lady nothing."

"Why did you go to the house?"

"I thought Karl was there and he'd help you. You're in trouble, innit? And I don't know what to do."

Lindy shook her head. "Can't trust nobody, not unless I say."

"Not even Karl?"

Lindy shrugged and pulled at the fish on her plate. "What was that old woman saying to you?"

"She's proper mad. Talks to herself. She gave me a chocolate bar and asked me about Mum and Dad. I lied."

"What do you mean?"

"I said Mum was a nurse and Dad was a postman and you were the best sister in the world. The last bit's true."

Sean blinked at her and fiddled with the Top Trumps cards strewn on his bed.

Lindy stared at him for a minute and then she started to giggle and soon they were both rolling about roaring with laughter, Lindy holding her sides as they started to ache. She threw a pillow at Sean and he picked it up and threw it back at her.

Jemma had loved it when they had pillow fights, Lindy remembered, as she dodged out of the way. She would pull herself up by the bars of her cot and jump up and down shrieking.

If Jemma had lived none of this would have happened. I would have been too busy to let Colin drag me into his illegal business.

"Do you know what's in Colin's house?" she asked Sean, as he lay panting on his bed. He looked very pale and she worried he might have an asthma attack.

"Spliffs."

She gave a short laugh. "Do you even know what a spliff is?"

"Terrence showed me how to roll them for him. I tried one once but it made my asthma worse."

Giving a joint to a nine-year-old with asthma! She felt like exploding as she looked at Sean's peaky face, his eyes wary.

Whatever happens, I have to get away from everything

and everyone to do with drugs. Who knows what Colin might do next? What if he gets Sean to run his filthy errands? I couldn't save Jemma but I won't have little Sean in prison.

It's up to me. I'll find Karl tomorrow. He has to help me now. It's an emergency.

In the morning, Lindy went downstairs, still worried. Her biggest problem was going to be getting into school without being spotted by one of the teachers. One thing was certain; she was never going back. She'd burnt her uniform and anyway she was about to betray Colin to the police. Once Colin was safely locked up, she had decided she was going to take Sean and run away so that they could start a whole new life together without their stupid family. *We'll go to Southampton or maybe London, get a flat. I've got enough money to get started and then I'll get a job.*

There was a note on the floor by the front door with her name on it. *Meet me today at 12 at the house. C.*

He must have pushed the note through the door this morning before anyone was up. What did he want now?

But first of all she had to drop Sean at the junior school and see him into class to make sure he stayed out of trouble. That took ages. Sean dragged his feet, complaining all the way. Then she had to cross town to get to Park Road. By the time she arrived at her school it was form time and everyone was in their classrooms. One or two stragglers remained in the corridors, but no one she knew to talk to.

Where was Karl's form room? She headed down the corridor towards the Special Unit when she suddenly stopped. *No, of course Karl won't be in there. He's a geek, a nerd, a boffin, reeling off facts and speaking like the real Prince William. He isn't a retard; he's probably the next Prime Minister.*

"Looking for Karl?"

Lindy whirled round. Jess was standing behind her, twirling her finger in her newly-dyed hair. Lindy stared at the red highlights. "I see the axe murderer finally found you."

"Ha ha," said Jess in a monotone. "So are you?"

"Who wants to know?"

"No wonder the teachers hate you. You can't answer even the simplest questions."

Lindy had to clench her fists to keep herself from slapping Jess. Instead she shouldered her hard to one side. Lindy was about to stride away when the bell went and the corridor filled with noisy teenagers swinging huge bags. Jess joined a little group of girls with Sarah and said something to them behind her hand. They all looked at Lindy and laughed.

"What?" she said.

"Just about Karl," said Jess.

"What do you know about Karl?"

"Only what he told me," said Jess and she walked off arm-in-arm with the others, all hooting with laughter and clutching each other like drunks on a Saturday night.

Karl wouldn't speak to a slapper like her. He only speaks to me, he said so.

And you believed him? whispered a little voice in her ear.

Chapter 22
Delivery

She needed to find Karl and the only place to ask was the school office. But the secretary, Mrs Jones, was so nasty that everyone hated her, even the teachers.

"Where's your uniform, Lindy Bellows?" she called out in her witch-around-the-cauldron voice, as soon as she caught sight of Lindy in her jeans and T-shirt.

"I'm not in school today. The Social's coming round. My mum's not well."

Mrs Jones frowned at her but didn't comment. Instead she swivelled her chair anti-clockwise and started typing on a computer.

"I need to find Karl Reece, he's in Year 10," said Lindy to Mrs Jones' back. No response, just the infuriating tapping on the keyboard.

"Excuse me, anyone home?"

"He's not in," screeched the witch from behind her high-backed chair.

"Where is he?" *What does she mean, not in? Is he sick, have the police caught him with the gun?*

"He's gone to London with his parents. Now off you go, some of us have work to do."

Lindy turned and stormed out of the office in a fury.

So that's it! He goes off with his parents on a holiday. And he told Jess and not me. A mixture of anger and jealousy rose in her. *He's so totally not to be trusted. I was right the first time. He's a complete waste of space. Probably sipping cocktails in the Hilton, congratulating himself on escaping me. The saddo girl who cuts herself with razor blades.*

Lindy ran down the corridor past the Head's office. She could hear her name being called but she ignored it and burst out of school. It was almost eleven. She had to meet Colin at the greenhouse at midday.

It was already Wednesday and she had to find out what Colin's plans were for Thursday so that she could tip off the police. She felt pressure rising inside her and she imagined again the cutting and the blood flowing out, taking away the pain.

How could Karl betray me like this? If he'll speak to Jess he'll speak to anyone.

Her head swirled with angry thoughts all the way to the greenhouse.

When she reached the lane, all was quiet. No sign of Bag Lady or her little spaniel. Lindy let herself into the house. As soon as she opened the door, she saw Colin standing by the tallest plants, inspecting the leaves and putting them into small plastic bags.

"Crop's ready, Lindy."

He took out a little bottle of antiseptic gel, squeezed some onto a tissue and wiped his hands, carefully cleaning between his fingers.

He's totally insane, why didn't Garth see it before?

"Ready for harvest. I want you here all day Saturday to help, so get here early. Elf's coming over too."

She shuddered at the sound of Elf's name.

Then Colin handed her a roll of notes. "Here, have a good night out and give that little brother of yours a cut."

She took the money. It felt good in her hand, thicker than usual. *How much? Is it enough to get away from you and your filthy world?*

"You've been a good girl, Lindy. Knew I could trust you." He went to the door, "OK, as you're here, you're coming."

Startled, she practically shouted, "Where?"

"Delivery," said Colin tapping on his Blackberry. "Come on, ain't got time to waste."

Her heart sank as she realised there was no escape and she followed him out to the car. They pulled out of the lane, the car roof firmly shut; Colin said he didn't want any dust in the car. Lindy saw Bag Lady standing by the field with the water trough, Prince William jumping around at her feet. Lindy slumped down in her seat, but she was sure Bag Lady had spotted her. She might be half-mad, but she must realise something weird was going on.

They swept onto the main road and Lindy decided to ask Colin about the boat, see if she could find out where he kept *Trojan 3*.

"Do you ever go sailing Col?"

"Been once or twice. Why?"

"A friend asked me to go, but I don't know if I'd like it."

"It's all right, when the sea's flat."

"Garth said I should try it, once at least. He gets seasick."

Colin laughed. "Yeah, I remember when we went out together. He only lasted about an hour, begged me to take him home."

"Where was that then?"

"Chichester Harbour, not far." Colin lit a cigarette and propped his right arm on the open window.

"So, was that in your own boat?" She gazed out of the window, pretending she didn't really care.

"Why do you want to know?" Colin's voice hardened into his familiar tone.

A frisson of fear went through her. *Mustn't make him suspicious.*

She changed the subject. Dragging a hand through her hair, she said, "First thing I'm going to spend that money on is a makeover!"

"Yeah, right," said Colin and he flicked his cigarette out of the window. They didn't speak again until they reached a small village, miles outside town. Colin drew up in front of a large, detached house, with a semi-circular drive where two matching SUVs were parked. Without speaking he unlocked a compartment under the steering wheel and pulled out several of the small plastic packets. He handed them to Lindy.

"Ring the doorbell three times and then knock twice. A bloke will open the door and hand you an envelope. You give him the stuff."

She started to speak, but he suddenly slammed his hand over her mouth and squeezed it into a tight O with his fingers. "Do it!"

She felt like screaming, "No!" But she didn't dare.

The walk to the front door felt like miles, her legs heavy with fear and worry. She did as Colin had told her. A tall young man, wearing a crumpled T-shirt and jeans, feet bare, still rubbing sleep from his eyes, opened the door. He silently handed her a fat brown envelope, before taking the packets from her.

This is me, Lindy Bellows, Class-A drug dealer. What happened to changing my name to Lindy Minogue and becoming a paramedic, saving people on my motorbike?

I've only got until tomorrow to break free for ever.

Chapter 23
Diagnosis

As Lindy arrived home she could hear her parents talking to someone in the front room. It was too early for Sean to be home from school. Pushing open the living room door, her heart did a flip. Karl was sitting on the one good armchair, sipping a mug of coffee, and her dad was saying in a polite voice, "You going to college then, son?"

"Yes," Karl answered, and Dad nodded as if he had these kinds of conversations all the time and even Mum had changed into an old cardigan and jogger bottoms, instead of her grubby dressing gown. She was offering Karl a cigarette.

What's he doing here? What's he told Mum and Dad? He'd better not have brought that gun back.

Lindy glared down at Karl and said, "Didn't know you smoked?"

Karl jumped to his feet and shook his head.

Lindy snapped at her parents, "We're going upstairs."

Karl nodded and smiled and then followed Lindy to the top of the house. Lindy slammed her bedroom door shut and jammed a chair under the handle.

"How could you? Just run away to London with Mumsy? Too much for you was it, being with the family from hell?" hissed Lindy.

177

"No! Lindy, I didn't. It was my parents."

"Oh, grow up."

"Please. Listen. It wasn't like that." Karl sat on her bed, his eyebrows concentrated in such an appealing line that Lindy relented and flung herself down onto Sean's bed.

"You've got one minute."

"My parents made me go to London. We went last night. Had to stay in this stupid hotel. Then this morning I had to see a psychiatrist. They think I have problems." Karl threw her a nervous look. "I didn't want to go. We just got back and I came straight here."

"Yeah, right, a trip to *London*? You must have *hated* it."

"You have to believe me." Karl's eyes were fixed on hers, his face anxious. "I didn't want to go."

Is he scared we won't be friends any more? No, I can't believe he cares that much.

Karl dragged a hand across his face and said, "Look, they told me to choose. Go and see this special doctor in London, or go away somewhere with them again, somewhere with a horrible jungle."

Lindy gave a snort. Karl started to lower his head into his chest but Lindy snapped, "So, did you talk?"

Karl shook his head.

Exasperated, Lindy yelled, "So what happened, you muppet!"

Karl said in a quiet voice, "The shrink said I was clever."

"How did he know that?"

"Got all the written tests right."

"So why didn't you speak?"

"Because of my parents. I hate them." His eyebrows knit into a fierce line.

Lindy gave a sarcastic snort. "You shot your mouth off on Monday all right."

"I thought you'd killed yourself."

They were silent for a minute. Lindy straightened the sheet in Jemma's cot and Karl stared at his boots.

Then Karl said, "I'm a mute, Lindy."

"You're a what?"

The tone of Karl's voice had changed and Lindy recognised it as his I-love-facts voice; deeper and more serious, as if he was reading the news on TV.

"A mute is someone who demonstrates a consistent failure to speak. You can be mute for physical reasons, maybe because you are deaf or born without a voice box."

"I thought you were deaf when I met you."

Karl nodded. "Everyone at Park Road thinks that. But, actually, I'm a Progressive Mute. I stopped speaking at home after... after Musa. Then I stopped speaking everywhere. It becomes like a phobia for some people, almost a fear of the sound of your own voice and then..."

"Then you couldn't start again."

Karl nodded. "Until the shock."

"So it was a good thing I cut myself?"

Karl reached out and took her hand. He licked his lips and looked around the room as if it was almost too much

179

to speak. Then he whispered, "It was the worst thing I've ever seen."

Worse than Musa's death?

She let him hold her hand, enjoying the warmth. The silence in the room seemed to stretch into eternity and she wanted it to go on and on. Karl's head was bent and she couldn't see his face, couldn't imagine what he was thinking. But his hand stayed firmly around hers, as if he too didn't want to break the moment. Then he seemed to change his mind and he slid his fingers free.

"I got you a present," he said in a shy voice. He pulled two new mobile phones from his pockets. "Now we won't lose touch again."

Karl was looking into her eyes and their heads moved closer and closer together until their lips were almost brushing. Lindy remembered how Liam used to kiss her, just grab her roughly and push his mouth against hers. If she was honest she didn't like kissing, not with Liam anyway.

But Karl will be soft, so soft. Only once he's kissed me, will he dump me?

She pulled back and said, "Show me this phone, then."

A look of disappointment crossed Karl's face and he lowered his head.

Lindy felt a deep disappointment too and to cover up her feelings she said, "Now I can text you when you go missing."

Karl looked up with relief and began taking the phones out of their boxes.

"Whose numbers do you want to put in?" he said. "I've already put my number in for you."

She couldn't think of anyone and then she said, "I'll get Garth's phone." She went off and when she came back Karl was tapping the keys.

"Who are you texting?" she said.

"Jimmy."

"Who?"

"Jimmy, the friend I told you about. He's deaf," said Karl in a tense voice. "He's like you."

"You what?"

"He doesn't care if I don't speak, either."

Karl was staring at her and Lindy ducked her head, fiddling about with the cot again. She wished she could enter Jimmy and Karl's silent, mysterious world, signalling to each other like deep-sea divers.

"I can't think of anyone deaf at school," she muttered.

Karl gave a snort. "He's not at school, he works at one of the boatyards. Everyone knows Jimmy."

It was like a light had switched on in her head. "Can Jimmy sail?"

"Course; sail, drive a motorboat, kayak…"

Lindy leapt to her feet. "We have to find him! I need a boat to get to Colin's boat out in the harbour. Come on! I'll explain on the way!"

"He's not there. He's staying with his auntie in Portsmouth until tomorrow."

Lindy slumped back on the bed. *Is this nightmare never*

*going to end? I have to wait until tomorrow to start searching
for Colin's boat? Tomorrow is Thursday!*

A sound started up, the theme tune to *The Simpsons*.
She looked round puzzled and, seeing Karl grinning at her,
suddenly realised it was her mobile phone. She grabbed
it from Sean's pillow, slid up the top and gazed at the
flashing screen.

"Press the green button," said Karl.

Lindy obeyed and, putting the phone to her ear, heard Karl
say, "We need to go out." He was holding his phone to his ear.

"Where?"

"Gotta buy a suit."

"What for?"

"Got an interview at Portsmouth Grammar School on
Monday. I rang up and pretended I was my dad. I want
to make a fresh start, Lindy, speaking like everyone else.
The Grammar School don't know about my mutism and
I'm going to make sure they never find out."

Lindy was silent for a moment.

"Will you come?"

*Nothing else I can do until Jimmy gets back, and I need to
fill Karl in. He must help me; he's got to.*

"OK," she said, and slid her phone shut.

They went downstairs and straight out of the house
before Lindy's parents could talk to them. Karl started up
the bike and they drove to town, drawing up outside a
smart menswear shop on the high street.

She watched Karl pick out jackets and trousers, the

young fitter measuring every inch of Karl's slight body.

Amazing what a credit card can get you.

"That's enough," said Karl. "I'll take it and that shirt." He pulled out his card, hassled the fitter to pack everything quickly and picked up the bags.

As they stepped out of the shop a voice said, "Hey Karl, fancy meeting you here." It was Jess.

Lunchtime and half the school would be on the high street heading for the chip shop. *Why does that cow have to turn up right now?*

Jess put her hand on the bag and peered inside. "Ooh, expensive, going to a party? Am I invited?"

Karl shrugged and ducked his head.

Embarrassed? Or flattered?

Jess was wearing a crisp white short-sleeved shirt, unbuttoned to her cleavage and her grey school skirt was hiked up to show off her slender legs. The red highlights still shone in her hair and she was wearing thick, shiny lip gloss. *Wish I could afford to go to the hairdressers.*

"Wanna hang out for lunch?"

Karl shrugged again but Lindy saw a quick grin on his face. Jess was grinning back.

Walk away, you idiot. She thinks she's got you. Maybe she has.

Lindy remembered the moment in the bedroom, Karl's disappointed look as she ducked away from his lips.

"What would your Liam say if he saw you and Karl out together?" Jess said to Lindy, and Lindy felt herself go hot and red. She lowered her eyes. Karl just stood there. She wanted to yell at him, "Jess is only after your money."

Suddenly there was a beeping noise and Karl reached into his pocket and took out his mobile. It was a text. Karl read it and was about to slide the top down when Jess grabbed his hand with a little laugh and snatched the phone.

"We need to swap numbers so we can hang out, maybe go to that party." She tapped keys rapidly on Karl's phone and then, just as quickly, took out her own phone and called it from Karl's. It was all over in a flash.

"Cool," said Jess. "Now I can get you any time I want," and she took Karl's hand again and slowly put the phone back in his palm. Then she flashed a smug grin at Lindy and walked off towards the Park Road crowd gathering at the chip shop.

Unbelievable!

Lindy gave Karl a hard stare.

"What?" said Karl.

"She said you talked to her yesterday."

Karl's eyebrows forked into a deep frown. "No I didn't. No one in school knows I speak. Why did she say that?"

Lindy shook her head. "She's after you, can't you see? And now she's got your mobile number."

Karl just shrugged and Lindy said impatiently, "Let's go."

Lindy walked off down the high street and turned into a side street away from the crowds. As Karl caught her up she said in a low voice, "What about the gun?"

Chapter 24
Evidence

Karl looked around swiftly to see if anyone was listening. "Not here."

He grabbed her arm and led her back to the bike. Lindy could see Jess and Sarah crossing the road, arm-in-arm, chatting away.

Karl must see Jess is after him. How long before he rings her? She comes from the same sort of home as him, doesn't she? Own room, Spanish holidays, not like me. But what about the gun? He couldn't tell Jess about that, she'd call the police on her stupid little phone.

They climbed on the bike and drove towards the Island. But Karl turned off down a side road before the bridge and parked the bike near the beach.

"Come on," he said and strode off along the footpath behind a crumbling old building.

The path was deserted. To their left was a large pond with thick reeds around the edges. Lindy could hear the sounds of birds and other animals moving about inside the reeds. The sea opened out on their right again. On the far shore, in the distance, was a big hotel. Dad said that was where managers of companies went for conferences and there were always expensive cars driving across the bridge and turning left into the hotel car park.

"We'll go there sometime, with the Winnings," he was always saying. But they never did.

She hadn't seen this view of the Island before. The cannabis house was quite near to the hotel, she realised, down a narrow winding road and then into the lanes.

They reached a second pond where the reeds were even thicker and taller. Karl stopped and looked round to make sure they were alone. Then he pointed to the far end. "Over there," he said. "I waded through the lake – it's not very deep – and dropped the gun right into those reeds. No one will ever find it."

Lindy stared across the water. "Karl I..." She stopped. *I thought he wanted the gun for himself; of course he didn't, look at him.*

Karl was standing at the edge of the pond, silent as usual, his dark hair blowing over his face in the breeze. He looked a thin, lonely figure. *Karl breaks the law a little bit but he wouldn't do any harm. He's just getting back at his parents. He's not a proper criminal, like everyone in my family.*

"That was so dangerous," she went on, "running off with the gun. What if the police had stopped you?" She looked straight into his eyes, staring hard as if she could see into his mind and read all the thoughts he'd been saving up for two silent years. *His brain must be bursting with stuff.*

Karl didn't answer but he held her stare without blinking. She nearly leaned forward to finish the kiss they'd almost started earlier, but she knew she couldn't handle it if he turned away, if she'd just imagined he felt like she did towards him. Then it would be like Liam leaving all over again. Love gone sour, spoilt, because she was too stupid to read the right signals. Liam was never coming back.

"You're in real trouble, aren't you?" said Karl.

Lindy didn't speak.

"Is it time to go to the police?"

A chill of horror ran through her. Jail for years and years, perhaps for ever. The thought was so awful that she covered her face with her hands and let out a moan.

Karl grabbed her arm. "What's really going on, Lindy?"

He pulled her over to a bench and in a low voice she told him everything.

"That's why I need a boat. To find *Trojan 3* and get all the evidence against Colin and Elf. Then I can tip off the police. There's some sort of big drugs deal tomorrow and the information is all on a computer on Colin's boat."

"But why not just go to the police anyway?" asked Karl.

"Isn't it obvious? I'm in too deep now. Colin and Elf have made sure of that. I've been growing a field of cannabis, my fingerprints are all over that stupid house. And Colin made me deliver cocaine and collect the money. The courts hate my family; they'll send me to prison for ever."

"But Colin made you do it."

"I'm a Bellows; my entire family are bent. Who would believe me? Anyway, Colin has too many evil friends, Garth warned me. If I go to the police, he'll know, and then there'll be no hiding place. Elf shoots people he doesn't like, Karl."

She nodded towards the pond where the gun lay rusting under the water in the reeds.

She got up and started to walk towards the road.

"Where are you going?"

"To the house. I don't want Colin getting suspicious." She stood for a minute looking back at Karl. He was staring out across the water. The bag with the suit was at his feet. *That's what it's all about for him. His new suit and his grammar school.* Suddenly she could see their different futures spread out in front of her. Karl would go to uni and become a famous inventor or engineer and she would go to prison, scrub floors and get her head kicked in.

She turned on her heels and strode away. As she reached the main road she heard the sound of a motorbike engine. *He'll just drive past*, she thought, and stepped out of the way. But the sound of the engine lowered to a putter and Karl drew up alongside her.

"Can I leave the suit at your house first? Don't want any awkward questions at home. They still don't know I'm going to try and stay here."

"Why Karl? Walk away now."

"You told me the answer yourself."

"What?"

"Who needs the police? Who needs any of them – teachers, shrinks, parents? They all tell you what to do, but they never listen."

Lindy looked at him in amazement and then she realised.

Karl gets it, what I'm having to deal with here. It was the first time she'd felt a surge of happiness in months. Not since she first had the greenhouse job and Colin had told her she was the one he wanted. *Karl wants to help me, he really wants to be with me.*

Her face broke into a grin and she said, "Sure, you can hang the suit in my wardrobe. That'll be a first in our house."

They climbed back on the bike and Karl revved the engine on full throttle before taking off.

At Lindy's house, they managed to sneak in and up to her room without her mum seeing.

"How's this?" said Lindy, pushing hangers to one side in the wardrobe. "Will it be OK here?" She looked at him anxiously.

"Yeah, that's great." Karl lifted the suit out of the bag and hung it on the rail.

"We'll be really careful with it," she said nervously. "I'll keep the door shut and I'll tell Sean to keep his hands off." She thought how often Sean's hands were sticky or grubby.

"Don't worry Lindy, it'll be fine," said Karl, smiling at her. "The interview's on Monday."

"What about your parents?"

"They're planning to drive to Africa next week. They don't seem bothered about me now they've got a diagnosis. But I'm not going with them. I'm sick of travelling."

Lindy looked at her watch. "I have to go, Colin expects me to check the house every day. I can't let him get suspicious now."

"I'll give you a lift," said Karl and they went back downstairs and out of the house to the bike.

They drove through town and over the bridge to the Island. Karl stopped the bike at the top of the lane. "Sure you want to go in?"

Lindy nodded and got off. "I'll be out in an hour."

"I'll wait out of sight."

The house was steaming as she let herself in. She was watering the plants upstairs when she heard the sound of a key in the lock. Peering over the banister, to her horror she saw both Colin and Elf coming into the house. They were talking in loud, angry whispers.

She couldn't make out everything but she heard the words, "snotty kid" and "back to the boat tonight".

"There's my girl," cried out Colin, spotting her on the stairs, and he gave Elf a meaningful nod.

Elf loomed over Colin, his pointed ears more marked under the powerful lamps. His hand was in his suit pocket.

Is he holding a gun? Lindy struggled to keep her voice steady. "I... I wasn't expecting you." She looked from Colin to Elf and then lowered her eyes. "Either of you."

"You'll be seeing a lot of us from now on, babes," said Colin grinning at her and giving Elf a nod. "We'll be here all the time, sorting this little lot out." He nodded towards the plants.

That's all I need. But she kept her eyes lowered and said nothing.

Colin went on, "There was some old woman outside,

said she'd seen a kid hanging around yesterday. You seen him? Only Elf's lost something valuable."

"No," she said quickly. Elf gave her a strange look. "What have you lost?"

Elf wouldn't recognise Sean, would he? Bag Lady better keep her mouth shut.

"None of your business," snapped Elf. Turning to Colin, he said, "Ready for Saturday?"

"Yes, yes. Lindy'll be here too." Colin raised an eyebrow at Lindy, who nodded.

"She'd better be," said Elf.

They walked off to the back of the house talking quietly. Lindy couldn't make out what they were saying. As she swept the floor her heart was beating like a drum. How much longer could she stand being in the same house as these two lunatics? *If I put a foot wrong, Elf will shoot me. That's what Garth said. I must make sure Sean never comes near them again.*

"Laters, babes," Colin called out, startling her and she nearly tripped over a wire snaking across the floor.

Then they were gone. But it was impossible to relax. They could come back any minute, Colin had made that clear. Lindy finished her jobs as quickly as she could and let herself out into the lane. It was a warm, sunny evening and as she walked up to the main road she looked round hopefully for Karl.

Suddenly a voice called out, "Doing the garden?" It was Bag Lady and she was carrying Prince William.

Startled, Lindy said, "What's it to you?"

"Prince give the little boy a nip but he wasn't bleeding. No need for the police, is there?"

The woman was peering up at her and Lindy could see an anxious look in her eyes. So she was scared of the police too.

"I won't tell if you don't. But keep away from the house. It belongs to my uncle. He hates dogs. I don't know what he might do to that." She nodded at the dog.

The woman gripped the dog tighter. "Is he the one with the fair hair, your uncle? Has a big car?"

"Just keep away," warned Lindy. "Don't mess with him or he'll set the police on you." Then, just to be sure, she added, "They take away dangerous dogs."

Why doesn't she do us all a favour and drop dead.

Chapter 25
TXTNG

Karl was waiting at the top of the lane.

"Jimmy texted. He'll be back in the morning. He thinks he can get us a boat."

"OK, that's good," Lindy was looking over her shoulder, worried that Bag Lady was still snooping around.

"So I thought..." Karl started and then stopped and ducked his head.

"What?" she said.

"Thought we could have a barbecue on the beach this evening. You know, hang out together a bit?"

She couldn't help feeling pleased, and was about to say yes, when Karl's phone bleeped.

He checked the screen. "It's a text from Jess."

Lindy snorted and Karl gave her a puzzled look.

How dumb can you get, even if the shrink says you're a genius. Jess is after you. Don't you get it? But she didn't want Karl to see how she felt. So she shrugged and said, "What does she want?"

Karl scrolled down, reading the text. "It says, 'My dad has a boat. I can take you out in it tomorrow.' But how—"

How does she know we need a boat tomorrow? Is she stalking us?

193

"Oh," said Karl, scrolling through his phone, "I sent her the same one I sent Jimmy earlier about needing a boat. I'm an idiot – I didn't realise it had sent. Well, it's good to know isn't it, Lindy? Might be useful."

He was waiting for her to say something and she couldn't say what she really felt – that maybe Jess would steal him from her before she had a chance. Or that maybe Karl had sent that text on purpose.

She shrugged and said, "Hang out with her if you want."

Karl gave her a startled look and then dropped his head, his hair flopping forward into his eyes. "I don't care about Jess, she's horrible. I've seen her getting at you."

That felt better; maybe he wasn't getting hooked in by Jess.

"Let's go to the beach, I've got something to show you," said Karl.

"What?"

He gave her a small smile. "It's a surprise."

She wasn't sure then. Surprises were usually something frightening, like Sean pulling Elf's gun out of a plastic bag.

"A good surprise," said Karl.

She relented, mostly because she didn't want Karl's thoughts to turn back to Jess. "Yeah, OK. But I'd better ring the neighbours, leave a message for Sean. Don't want him to come looking for me like yesterday."

They drove to the supermarket and bought some food and a disposable barbecue. Then Karl took them to the houseboat where they'd stayed the other night. He had fixed a padlock to the front door and, producing a key, he unlocked it and walked in. Before Lindy had crossed the threshold, Karl had switched on two large fluorescent strip torches.

"You moving in?"

"Considering it. Have to live somewhere when I go to the Grammar. This is handy for the ferry."

"What if the owners come back?"

"I'll make them an offer."

Lindy couldn't help asking, "Will your parents let you?"

"What do I care?"

Lindy gave a snort, but she couldn't help grinning as she helped carry the stuff to the beach.

Soon there was the smell of chargrilled burgers and sausages wafting over them. When they were almost full, Karl stuck marshmallows on wooden sticks and they sat roasting them on the hot coals. The sun was dipping low in the sky, spreading broad swathes of red across the long strips of cloud. The sea lay like a flat, calm sheet over the bay.

Karl handed her a Coke and Lindy tipped it up, the fizz tickling her nose. She was feeling very content and comfortable and, looking over at Karl, she said, "Ever been to the fair at Southsea?"

"No one to go with."

"I love rides, scarier the better. Dad's going to take us to Alton Towers next time he gets a win."

"Nice," said Karl with a grin.

Music was streaming out over Karl's iPod speakers and Lindy watched as his long, narrow fingers played air guitar over his chest. She felt a huge urge to kiss him on each eyebrow. *What would he do?*

They lay side-by-side, not speaking until it grew dark and the sound of the gulls had completely died away. It was a very still night with a bright moon.

Then she said, "Why did you follow me last Friday?"

"Dunno. I was just riding around, and I saw you go into the lane."

"So?"

"I thought," Karl hesitated. "I thought, after the bullies on the basketball court, I thought..."

"What?"

"You were like me."

"Yeah, right."

There was a silence and then Karl said, "Alone, like me."

The second silence lasted a very long time. Lindy didn't feel like speaking ever again.

Then Karl said, "I went up to the house but I couldn't see anything through the window. The curtains are very thick."

"So you broke in." Lindy gave a short laugh.

"I wanted to see if I could."

"I could have called the police. Weren't you scared?"

"No!" Karl yelled and Lindy almost dropped the can she was clutching. Karl threw himself to his feet and turned to look down at her, his face dark with rage. "I don't care. The rules don't apply to me."

Lindy stared at him standing on the beach in his bare feet, jeans hanging low off his hips, the waistband of his boxers exposed.

"Rules suck," she said and raised the can to her lips.

He turned away for a minute and when he turned back there was a look of such tenderness on his face that she had to crouch down by the fire and sprinkle it with sand so that he wouldn't see her cheeks burn red.

Karl picked up the remains of the food and went up the steps into the houseboat. Lindy followed and watched as he made up the sofa bed. There was no line of cushions tonight. She slipped off her jeans and lay down next to the wall. Karl fussed around a little, locking the door and switching off the torches. Lindy watched as he took off his jeans.

"You could leave the candle for a bit," she said.

Karl nodded, standing silently over her, the left side of his face shining in the candlelight. Then he pulled off his T-shirt and lay down beside her, very close, his arms seeking her body.

They lay in silence for a long time, Karl's bare skin warm through her top, his familiar salty smell clean and fresh in the dark room.

Then he whispered, "Ever been to Paris?"

"No, what for? Doesn't have any rides."

They burst into silent laughter, feeling the delicious shake of each other's bodies. *We prefer silence,* Lindy thought, and she closed her eyes as Karl kissed her on the lips.

Chapter 26
Slow Motion

Her name was being called, but it was underwater and she was in the sea with Karl, except he was a fish with big popping eyes. *It's all right for him, he can swim, but I'm drowning,* and gasping for breath she fought her way to the surface and woke up. A grey light showed through the open door and she reached across the bed. She was alone. *Where's Liam?* But then she remembered. It wasn't Liam, it was Karl.

"Do you want to?" Karl had whispered last night, his finger stroking her cheek.

But she couldn't, not again. What if Karl walked away afterwards, like Liam had? She hadn't answered, just shook her head slowly against his chest. He didn't ask again and they had fallen asleep to the sound of water dragging over the pebbly beach.

But now she felt shy as she pulled on her jeans and stepped outside the houseboat. She spotted him down at the water's edge, wearing only his boxer shorts and T-shirt. *He's got really hairy legs,* she thought and she giggled loudly. Karl turned and she called out, "What time do you call this?"

"Sunrise. Best time of the day."

"You're insane."

"Never said I wasn't."

Wow, he's even telling jokes now. Lindy ran down the steps and bustled about gathering driftwood for a fire. The sun climbed above the horizon, promising another warm day. *A good day for sailing. We'll find Colin's boat, I just know it,* she thought, and a happy feeling washed through her as she sipped a mug of hot tea.

"Jimmy will be back early this morning," Karl said. "I thought you'd want to see him as soon as possible." He reached across to throw another stick on the fire, and his hand brushed against her knee. Their eyes locked for a second and then he looked away.

She stretched out her hands and warmed them for a few minutes by the fire and then she said, "I need to go home first and make sure Sean is OK."

Karl nodded and they tidied up, locked up the houseboat, and set off through the Island. Karl had texted Jimmy to meet them at Lindy's house. "He has a 1953 Triumph with a sidecar. It's a classic. He'll take you for a ride, if you like," Karl told her.

Sounds risky, and anyhow he's deaf. How on earth am I supposed to speak to him?

Jimmy was sitting astride a huge black bike when they arrived in Gull Terrace. The bike looked out of place in the tatty street. Lindy had imagined a small, wizened old man, with a glazed look and hearing aids sticking out of his ears. But Jimmy was over six foot, with pale, fleshy arms folded across his broad chest. His light brown hair was cut short and he wore a black T-shirt and frayed jeans cut off above the ankles. His bare feet had been pushed into battered trainers. When Jimmy saw Karl he started signing rapidly, grinning broadly.

"Er, any chance of a translation?" said Lindy.

"He wants to know who the babe is," said Karl.

"Charming," said Lindy, but she gave Jimmy a winning smile. *He's my key to Colin's secrets. Have to keep him sweet.* "You two wait here while I go and make sure Sean is OK."

Lindy let herself quietly into the house and ran upstairs. The bedroom was empty and seemed to be more of a mess than usual. An inhaler lay discarded on Sean's pillow. Lindy picked it up and shook it. It was a new one. Did that mean he'd gone out without his puffer? Suddenly scared, she ran into the bathroom and then around the rest of the house. No sign of Sean anywhere. Thundering back upstairs she threw open her parents' bedroom door.

"Where's Sean?" she yelled.

Her father lay snoring on his back, but her mother opened a bleary eye. "Said he was going to find you at Colin's. He'll be home soon, sure enough," she muttered.

Sean has gone to the greenhouse again. Oh my God! Colin made it clear he and Elf could turn up there any time from now on. They're checking the stupid crop, or something.

Lindy ran downstairs and outside, calling to Karl, "Come on, we have to get to the house."

"Why, what's the problem?"

"I think Sean's gone over there. What if he bumps into Colin and Elf? We can't risk it."

Karl signed to Jimmy, they both fired up their bikes and Lindy jumped on behind Karl. They headed off towards the Island. *I'm going to lock Sean in his room until this is over,* Lindy thought as they crossed the bridge over Langstone harbour and turned down to the lane. When they arrived she saw a silver Jag parked outside the house. The front door was open.

"Sean!" she cried out as she jumped off the bike and ran towards the house.

"Be careful, Lindy, wait for me," shouted Karl, running up behind her.

But Lindy shoved the door wide open, and, to her horror, saw Elf, his arm locked tight round Sean's neck. He was yelling at Sean, "What you doing hanging around here, you little punk? You trying to break into my car again?"

"Let him go, I'll kill you!" Lindy screamed, but Elf pushed past her, punching Karl out of the way and dragging Sean with him.

Karl let out a grunt and crumpled to the floor. Lindy ran past him, just in time to see the Jag reverse and whip round, tyres screeching. Sean's face appeared at the back window, hands banging on the glass, his mouth open in a scream. Elf swerved past them back up to the main road.

Karl was on his feet, swaying slightly, hand to his mouth.

"We have to follow them," shouted Lindy, tugging him towards the bike.

Karl hesitated for a second, then he nodded to Jimmy and they mounted their bikes, Lindy scrambling up behind Karl. She thought her heart would burst out of her chest as they roared back up towards Langstone Bridge. The road was still empty in the early morning and the Jag swerved slightly as it picked up speed on the straight.

He's heading for the motorway, we'll never catch him then. What will he do to Sean?

An image of Elf shooting Sean and tossing his body out of the car swum in front of Lindy's eyes and she swayed to one side, almost losing her balance. The tarmac raced beneath her and her ears were deafened by the noise of the engines.

Suddenly, there was a tremendous surge of throttle from behind and Jimmy overtook them, weaving to and fro in front of the Jag.

He's trying to stop Elf picking up speed beyond the bridge.

Jimmy's bike almost leapt in the air and, just as she was convinced he was about to crash, they neared the end of the bridge. Jimmy jammed on his brakes and, skidding round, planted his huge bike in the centre of the road. With a squeal of tyres, Elf swerved hard right towards the sea. The morning tide was just turning, the water still high below the quayside.

Karl stood upright and threw his bike after the Jag, bumping over the potholed surface, nearly throwing Lindy off as she stood up too, her whole body shaking with fear and the vibrating engine.

"We're too close," screamed Lindy as she gripped Karl tightly. She felt his shoulders clench as he swerved past Elf's bumper, missing by centimetres. Sean's face, white with terror, flashed past her for a second and then she heard a loud crack.

A gun?

But there was no time to look back. The ground was rapidly disappearing beneath their tyres.

Stop! Stop now! thundered through Lindy's head.

Then they were flying through the air, the bike dropping away beneath them. Lindy's body was thrown sideways into the cold, grey water and, as she plunged beneath the surface, arms flailing, she caught sight of the machine falling like a blown leaf beside her. No sign of Karl anywhere.

Chapter 27
Silence

Lindy sank in the cold water, her lungs bursting, the salt making her gag. Then she felt her feet touching the muddy harbour bed. She was drowning and no one was there to save her. She tried to wave her arms and legs, kicking desperately to rise to the surface, but all she could see was mud swirling around her. The dark, cloudy water held her in its grip and panic froze her limbs.

Where was Karl? He can swim, can't he? He could come and save me, couldn't he? Then everything seemed to go very dim. Lindy felt her arms and legs go limp and her mind clouded over as if she was sinking into a dream. A nice warm dream where everything was sorted and she didn't have to worry any more.

I'll be a fish; I'll swim away from everyone into this silent world. Karl's world. Must be OK if I'm in Karl's world.

It was very quiet at the bottom of the sea, like the silence when Karl wasn't speaking. There was also a muffled roaring in her ears, like the roar of the bike when she clung to Karl's back and words were just not necessary. *If I stop breathing will I find Karl?*

Then a huge arm, thick as a python, wrapped itself around her waist and her eyes jerked open with surprise.

She was rising, up and away from the fish and the mud and suddenly her head broke the surface and her eyes were stinging from the salt. Mouth open, choking and coughing, she felt herself towed forward and then pushed up from behind onto a hard, stone surface.

Sean's face, streaked with tears, appeared in front of her eyes, his hands scrabbling at her clothes as he helped Jimmy to heave her onto the quay. Spluttering and coughing, her lungs swollen with salt water, Lindy wondered whether asthma was like drowning. Someone rolled her onto her side and she felt her stomach heave. Sour, salty liquid splattered out and down her clothes.

"Her arms are all cold," Sean's voice wailed over her. "She's dead."

"She's alive," said another voice and, opening her eyes again, Lindy could see Karl lying next to her, soaking wet, blood trickling from his mouth onto the uneven stones of the quayside.

"Did Elf shoot you?" she whispered.

Karl's face was chalk white. "He fired, but he missed."

Jimmy was sitting on the ground crossed-legged, staring down at Karl with a worried frown on his face.

Jimmy saved us. But he brought Karl up first. I'm not first with anyone.

Colin's voice echoed in her head again, "You're the one that I want." What a thrill that had given her. But it was all a lie. He just wanted to trap her in his dirty, illegal underworld so that she could never escape.

Because of Colin, Karl had nearly been killed.

And you could have drowned, whispered a voice in her head. *Who would care?*

"You all right, Lindy?" asked Sean anxiously.

She looked up at him, bending over her. He was stroking her arm very gently, as if scared she would break.

Little Sean cares, doesn't he? Garth isn't here to look out for us any more. Do I have to take over now?

"I'm OK," she said, and sat up slowly. Elf's car had crashed into the side of the bridge as it skidded over the rough ground. The front wing on the driver's side was crumpled and glass from the windscreen had shattered into tiny shards all over the ground. The pieces winked like diamonds in the morning sunlight. She could just make out a ghostly white head, ears pointed, slumped over the steering wheel.

"Is he dead?" said Lindy.

"Hope so," muttered Sean.

Jimmy stood up and went over to the car. He found Elf's wrist and held it for a moment. Then he turned and signed to Karl.

"He's alive," said Karl. He signed again and Jimmy nodded. "I thanked him for saving us."

Lindy looked at Jimmy and nodded in agreement.

Sean picked up a rock and threw it at the car. It hit the still gleaming door, denting it below the handle.

Then Lindy remembered and, rounding on Sean, yelled, "What were you thinking, going round to Colin's house!"

"You didn't come back – I was scared!" Sean yelled back.

"I waited until after midnight, then I got Darren's bike and went to the house."

"You're mad!" cried Lindy. "You're completely nuts, you're worse than—"

"I thought they would shoot you," said Sean.

Lindy stared at Sean's grubby face, big shadows under his eyes from lack of sleep. His cheeks looked even more hollow than usual. He looked so small and helpless. She hadn't really noticed before, too absorbed in Jemma to worry about her little brother.

It's my job to keep him safe now, isn't it? I'm not letting him out of my sight again until Colin is locked up or dead!

As she stood up she thought she saw a curtain twitch in a window of the pub at the far end of the quay. "They've probably called the police," she said, nodding towards the building.

"We'd better go," said Karl, but he was still lying on the ground, looking very pale.

Then, in the distance, the faint sound of a siren floated over the morning air.

"Come on Karl, get up," said Lindy fiercely, pulling at his arm. "We can't let them find us, they'll take us in for questioning. There's no time." She looked at her watch but it was gone from her wrist, lost in the sea probably. She grabbed Sean's arm. "Give me your watch," and as he hesitated she snapped, "Now!"

"You go Lindy, make a run for it," said Karl. He was dabbing the blood at the side of his mouth.

"No way!" said Lindy. "We all go," She whirled round and pointed to Jimmy's bike, "on that."

Karl stared over at the bike for a minute, then turned to look at Jimmy. Lindy could hear the sirens getting nearer. Jimmy gave Karl a firm nod.

"OK," said Karl. "Get in the sidecar with Sean."

They squashed in, Sean on Lindy's lap, Karl, on the bike behind Jimmy. Then the engine exploded into life and Jimmy accelerated off, heading away from the roundabout, back across the bridge to the Island before the sirens reached the quayside.

We got away, they'll never know we were there. Lindy almost whooped out loud. She felt Sean settle on her lap and a memory of Jemma's warm body cuddled on her knees rushed in. If she closed her eyes she could almost believe they were sitting in front of the telly, Jemma laughing at her programmes. Jemma liked to wave TerryTed up and down and make Lindy sing along to all the silly tunes. Lindy had loved it.

Was this an 'every sad thought?'

Lindy put her arms around Sean and held him tightly to fill up the emptiness inside her.

Chapter 28
Mute

Jimmy drove them to Lindy's house but he wouldn't come in.

"He's shy," said Karl. "He won't want to meet your mum and dad."

Who would?

But Mum and Dad were still in bed. Lindy took Karl upstairs and found some of Garth's old clothes for him to change into, including a T-shirt which read, 'In The Future, We'll All Be Older.'

"Cool," said Karl as his phone bleeped. "It's a text from Jimmy. He's going to try and find us a boat."

Lindy heard the sound of the motorbike starting up in the road below. "Go and get changed in the bathroom," she told Sean, sending him out with a clean pair of jeans.

"Off to school is he?" said Karl.

"No way! He stays with us all the time, OK?" said Lindy with a frown.

Karl held his hands up. "OK by me. Safer that way."

Lindy gave a curt nod as Sean came back into the bedroom.

Then there was nothing to do but sit and wait. Karl and Sean started a game of Top Trumps. Lindy went down to make tea and sandwiches. She heard Mum getting up and going into the bathroom but there was so sign of Dad.

Back upstairs Karl was talking on the phone. "I'm not in school either... got an interview. Yeah, OK."

He clicked off the phone and gave Lindy a nervous glance. "That was Jess."

"What does *she* want?"

"She asked me if I wanted to go down to her dad's boat today."

"Isn't she at school? What's she playing at now?"

"Don't you see, Lindy? This could be the answer," Karl was talking quickly, willing her to listen. "We get Jess to lend us *her* boat. Jimmy just texted me, he can't get a boat anywhere."

"She can't come with us!"

Karl sighed. "What else can we do?"

Lindy dragged a hand across her eyes. It was nearly eleven. The hours were draining away like the tide and soon, very soon maybe, Colin was going to do a massive drugs deal and she still had no idea where or when and had nothing to tell the police. Assuming she could even safely give him away anonymously. And then she would take Sean and run and run and run.

They'd travel light of course; he couldn't take his toy cars. She'd already decided to take TerryTed and the little pink sheet from Jemma's cot. But really she just needed the cash in the box under her bed. They could hitch to Brighton, or maybe Jimmy would give them a lift on his bike. She rather liked the sidecar with Sean cuddled up on her lap. They could trust Jimmy, couldn't they? But what about Jess? *We'll have to risk it, there just isn't time.*

Lindy nodded. "OK. And you," she pointed at Sean, "you stay close and do what I tell you."

"OK, sis," said Sean, skipping across the room.

They went downstairs and out of the house. Jimmy was waiting for them on the main road. They drove to the marina at the top of the Island, behind the big hotel. It was full of huge, expensive-looking yachts.

Just the sort of place Jess's dad would keep a boat, like all the other rich people.

"He's going to ask one more person," said Karl, signing to Jimmy, who nodded and went over to an office building. "We need something small and fast, a motorboat, not a sailing yacht."

"Where did you learn to sign?" asked Lindy.

"Jimmy taught me."

"And he really knows how to sail?"

"He's worked with boats since he was twelve. He didn't go to school much, but he knows every inch of the water between here and the Isle of Wight. If anyone can find Colin's boat, Jimmy can. We just need deep water."

"How's that?"

"If the tide is out round Hayling, you can't get to the boats. We need high tide and then we must stick to the channels or we'll ground the boat. *And* we have to make sure we don't get stuck when the tide turns."

"What happens then?" asked Sean.

"The boat ends up in the mud and we have to sit tight and wait for high tide. It takes about eight hours."

Sean gave a low whistle and Lindy shivered. "Colin would be long gone by then."

Karl nodded. "It could take hours to find Colin's boat, there's so many places to look."

"What if we don't find it?"

"We will. Jimmy can find anything out here."

"You don't think he'll go to the police?"

"No way. Jimmy has only one law – his own."

Jimmy was gone a long time and Lindy paced around checking her watch every few minutes. Sean ran off down to the beach and was digging in the sand with a bit of wood, piling it up and marking out a ditch to fill up with seawater. But the tide didn't seem to be coming in.

Is it going out? Have we missed our one chance to find Trojan 3? Lindy wanted to scream out in frustration.

"So you came?"

It was Jess. She was walking towards them wearing very brief white shorts and a light green vest which ended above her pierced belly button. The skin on her belly was as tanned as her legs. Lindy could feel Karl straighten beside her as Jess came up.

Is he going to actually talk in front of her?

"No school, then?" said Karl.

Lindy sucked in her breath and folded her arms.

Jess raised her eyebrows, "Nice voice, big boy. I thought

you were the kid who doesn't speak."

Karl went red and looked at the ground, his dark hair flopping over his face.

Sean had run up and he broke into laughter. "Big boy, big boy," he called out, jumping round Karl.

"Shut it, you muppet," growled Lindy.

"What are you doing here and who's that little squirt?" said Jess, looking from Lindy to Sean. "Shouldn't you all be in school?"

"Shouldn't you?" Lindy snarled back.

Jess tossed her head. "Doctor's appointment. I'm off for the rest of the week. I've got to have blood tests." She looked quite pleased with herself.

Karl gave Lindy a warning look. "We need a boat, actually." He glanced over at Jimmy who was coming towards them, shaking his head. "To find a friend's boat. He's left something on it which he needs urgently."

Jess tipped her head on one side and said with a silly grin, "I thought it was just you and me, Karl."

In your dreams. Come on, come on, just say yes.

"Look, Jess," Karl tried again. "We really need your help. We've only got a couple of hours and we've got to find that boat. It's a matter of... of..."

"Life or death!" finished Sean dramatically, and jumped in the air with a fist pump.

Jess looked from Karl to Lindy for a minute and then her face broke into a grin. "Well, OK, if it's that important. But only if you and me do something later, Karl."

Karl ducked his head and Jess seemed to take that as a yes.

"Hector should let us take my dad's boat out. Maybe we could say it's for Geography." Jess called out to a man with greying hair, wearing a peaked navy blue cap and carrying a loudspeaker. He stopped and waited for them to come over.

"Who's this lot, then?" said Hector, eyeing them up suspiciously. Lindy glared back.

Then Karl spoke up. "I'm sure you know Jimmy, sir," he said, and to her astonishment Lindy watched Hector's expression change and he gave a grudging nod. Jimmy stood with his feet apart, arms folded, like a bodyguard. "He's an expert sailor and we wanted him to show us some of the coastal features of the Island for our Geography project."

Even Jess looked impressed.

"Does your dad know about this?" said Hector to Jess, eyeing Lindy and Sean closely.

He's going to ask us for ID in a minute.

"Oh yes Hector, of course, and we all know how good Jimmy is. We'll be perfectly safe."

"What about the little 'un?"

"I have to look after him, Mum's sick," muttered Lindy. Sean opened his mouth and she gave him a vicious kick before he could start.

"My parents trust me totally with Jimmy," said Karl.

The magic word: parents. Proper parents.

"The boat hasn't been out for a few weeks," said Hector, "so it would be good to start it up. Just for an hour, mind you."

Lindy's heart sank. How could they find Colin's boat in an hour?

"Oh come on, Hector," said Jess in a wheedling tone. "We won't get very far in an hour and I really need this for my coursework. You know what my dad's like about school stuff."

There was a pause while Hector stared round at the little group. Then a shout came from the shore. Hector turned, waved to someone launching a yacht, and turned back.

"Right then, it's just after twelve now. You'll be going out on the ebb tide, so you must be back before three." He held three fingers close up to Jimmy's face and Jimmy nodded, pointing to his watch and mouthing "three". Then Jimmy also held up three fingers to be absolutely clear.

"That's marvellous," said Karl, "thank you so much. We'll take good care of the boat and be back in plenty of time."

Bag Lady would love him now he's talking. He really sounds like Prince William.

Hector was clearly impressed as he led them towards the water, quizzing Karl about his Geography project. Lindy almost laughed out loud as she watched Karl blind Hector with an encyclopaedia-worth of facts.

The motorboat was quite small and they had to squash together on deck. Karl handed out orange life jackets, as Jimmy started the engine.

Hector was still shouting last-minute instructions as they cruised towards the mouth of the inlet. "Keep to the port side until you reach the open sea, you've got a sandbank to avoid.

And keep your distance from Thorney Island, the MoD don't like snoopers…"

"We'll be fine, don't worry about a thing," shrieked Jess, and then they were out of earshot and cruising forward, the swell of the boat already making Lindy feel sick.

Chapter 29
Military

"*Trojan 3, Trojan 3*", Lindy repeated to herself as they sped through the water. It's a motorboat, that much Garth had told her, but it would hardly have a big arrow pointing to it. *How on earth do you find a boat?*

She couldn't bear to look down at the water skimming beneath them. The near-drowning this morning was still too fresh in her memory. *Maybe we should just go home.*

Jimmy was steering with one hand and signing rapidly to Karl with the other. "Look at those two, nerdy or what?" Jess giggled.

"You asking for a slap?" said Lindy.

"Come on then."

But the boat felt like a live animal under her feet and she was terrified of standing up and falling overboard. Next to her, Sean was leaning right over the side, trying to trail his hand in the water. She grabbed the waistband of his jeans to keep him in the boat.

Why did Sean and Jess have to come? It would have been so much better with just Jimmy and Karl. We wouldn't have to speak at all.

"Are we nearly there?" cried out Jess in a childish voice.

"When are we having an ice cream?" Sean joined in.

"Shut it you two," said Lindy, "or I'll get Jimmy to chuck you overboard."

Jess snickered and narrowed her eyes at Lindy, "I don't think so," she said quietly, so that Karl wouldn't hear. Then she blew Jimmy a kiss and, to Lindy's amazement, Jimmy's cheeks went bright red.

Just as Lindy was considering getting up and striding over to Jess she felt the cool touch of Karl's hand on her arm. At that moment Jimmy swung the boat round the mouth of the inlet and Karl tipped forward, grabbing the railing as they entered the open water of Chichester Harbour and headed south. It was a cool, breezy afternoon and there were yachts criss-crossing the water in the distance.

"Where to?" asked Karl.

Lindy looked around her wildly. There was suddenly so much sea. *This is a nightmare.*

"What did Garth tell you?" said Karl quietly, one eye on Jess who was examining her nails.

"Just that the boat was a motorboat, Colin parked it off Hayling Island and it's called *Trojan 3*. Garth was seasick and they had to go back to shore in a rowing boat. The beach was quite stony and there were some rusty old boats dumped on the shore."

"Jimmy thought he'd work his way south, down the Hayling coast, going in and out of the inlets. They're good places to... er... keep a boat." Karl trailed off as Jess looked up.

"I suppose so," said Lindy, not even sure which way was

south. "If Colin has something planned for tonight we've only got a few hours."

"Three actually. Once the tide starts going out we have to get the boat back or we'll be beached out on the mud until nightfall."

"It's the sea – it's supposed to be full of water. We nearly drowned in it this morning!"

"Don't know much, do you?" said Jess.

Sean glared at her. "Lindy knows more than you."

"She knows nothing about the sea round here," said Jess, coolly. "The tide turns every eight hours and you have to know all the channels or you're dead." Sean flinched. "My Dad says the channels are all very narrow and if you make a mistake you can be stuck for ever and no one will come and rescue you. My Dad says—"

"Stuff your—" Lindy started, but Karl gently laid his hand on her arm and suddenly she just wanted to kiss him instead.

"No point in falling out now," said Karl in a low voice. "Jimmy will find the boat, I promise you."

Lindy slumped back down in her seat, holding her stomach. Sean settled down next to her, keeping his distance now from Jess who sat opposite, trying to catch Karl's eye.

"Feeling sick?" asked Karl.

Lindy nodded.

"The trick is to look at the horizon."

Lindy tried it and found that gradually her stomach settled down.

"I never get seasick," said Jess, coming over and pushing herself onto the bench between Lindy and Karl.

Lindy almost fell off. "Hey! Watch it!"

Jess gave her a smug grin and, draping herself over Karl's shoulder, said, "There's a party tonight, on the surfers' beach. Coming?"

"Thought you had blood tests," snapped Lindy, with a glare.

"Not at night time." Jess gave a laugh. "What about it, Karl?"

"Let's see how it goes, OK?" said Karl, his eyebrows knitting together.

That's what he does when you confuse him, stupid cow.

Jess smirked at Lindy and then she said to Karl, "You have the most amazing eyebrows. I could pierce the left one for you. Look really cool."

Karl shook her off gently and went over to stand next to Jimmy who was spinning the wheel, steering into a small inlet. Karl started to call out the names of dinghies and motor cruisers and Sean joined in.

Then Sean cried out, "There it is!"

Lindy got to her feet, looking around for any sign of Colin or Elf. *But Elf won't be here, he's probably out cold in hospital.*

Jimmy accelerated forward to a small cluster of boats. Lindy could just make out the letters T R... and a 3 in bold red paint. *This is it.* Jimmy suddenly veered left and came alongside.

Sean read out the name in disbelief, "*Triton 3!*"

"Good try, Sean," said Karl.

220

"So what are you looking for?" asked Jess.

Karl and Lindy exchanged looks and Sean fiddled with his shoelace.

"Well, if you don't tell me, I can't help, can I? Come on, Karl," said Jess in a wheedling voice, "you can tell me, can't you?"

If she carries on like this, I'll chuck her overboard myself.

But Karl said, "It's nothing really. Lindy's cousin left his laptop on the boat and he needs it."

"Why?" said Jess suspiciously.

"Oh you know, for business stuff. He's in a meeting today and we said we'd go and get it."

"Instead of going to school?" Jess was looking from Lindy to Karl.

There was a pause. Lindy could see Karl was trying to come up with a reason, when Sean said, "We don't go to school on Thursdays."

"Why not?"

"We have to see the Social Workers, we're a problem family..."

Jess sniggered and even Lindy had to suppress a smile.

"And Karl," Sean went on, "sees his special maths tutor. He's a boffin."

Jess turned to Karl, "You said you had an interview."

"Yeah, well, that too, they want me to do A levels early." Karl nodded.

"So our cousin rang us," said Lindy quickly, "and asked us to help. He knew we were all at home today."

Jess shrugged. "Typical Bellows family. Everyone out of work or in prison. No wonder the social workers keep an eye on you lot."

Lindy unfurled her spearnail but Karl put out a restraining arm.

"So come on Jess, keep looking," said Sean in a cheery voice and he stood up, almost tipping over the side.

They cruised on down the side of the Island towards the south end, past the boatyard near Sandy Point where Jimmy worked. Masses of boats were moored to brightly-coloured buoys bobbing in the sea. There were tall yachts, their shrouds chiming in the breeze and ocean-going motor cruisers, but no sign of Colin's boat.

A line of canoes appeared ahead of them, skirting the sandbanks off East Head.

"I used to go camping up there," said Jess. "We sailed from Hayling at night and played war games by torchlight. We sat up all night on the beach cooking sausages on campfires."

Sean's eyes widened in envy. "Can I come next time?"

"I'm a bit big for games," Jess said in a scornful tone. "Haven't been for years."

"I'm sending Sean to camp this summer," said Lindy.

"Wicked!" said Sean.

"It's not free, you know," said Jess, flicking her hair.

"I've saved up," snapped Lindy.

They had cruised right round the yacht club and in and out of the clusters of boats moored further out. It was nearly two o'clock and Jimmy began to sign towards Karl, pointing urgently at his watch.

"He says should we try the other side of the Island. Go back up to Langstone Bridge and over west to where the sewage works are. Maybe he keeps it down there."

Lindy shook her head, thinking of Colin's fanatical cleanliness. "Colin wouldn't go near a sewage works."

"That leaves the moorings around the far side of Thorney Island."

"No," said Jess. "We'd have to go close to the island and Hector told us not to. I don't want to get into any trouble."

"It's getting late," said Karl. "Jimmy thinks we should try."

"No, we can't. Please, Karl." The smug look Jess had worn all the time she'd been on the boat slipped from her face.

"We have to," said Lindy and she leaned over and pulled on Jimmy's arm, mouthing "please". She put her hands together as if she was begging him.

Sean, jumping up and down, joined in, "We have to! Please, Jimmy, please!"

The boat suddenly rocked and Jimmy lost his footing and just managed to grab the wheel in time. Lindy was thrown onto Jess and they both fell to the deck.

"Get off me!" yelled Jess, pushing Lindy so hard she banged her head on the side. "I wish I'd never let you come with us."

"Me too," muttered Lindy, rubbing her head.

Just then Jimmy spun the wheel and, giving Karl a curt nod, he turned the boat in a wide circle and cut back north towards the bottom end of Thorney Island.

Looking left, Lindy could see up the coast of Hayling Island which they'd just come down. *Where is it, where is Colin's boat? How much longer before Jess gets so suspicious she rings her dad? Or the police?*

As they reached Thorney Island, Lindy looked around, but there were no other boats near them and none moored near the shore. Jimmy eased back the throttle, reducing the engine to a low rumble, his eyes keenly scanning the coast.

This is a pebbly coast like Garth said; Colin's boat must be here somewhere.

Just then a voice boomed over a PA system: "TURN YOUR BOAT AROUND IMMEDIATELY. DO NOT APPROACH. MoD LAND. NO UNAUTHORISED PERSONNEL."

Chapter 30
Deep

Jimmy continued to steer towards the coastline and Sean whooped, calling out, "Way to go, Jim man!"

"Don't be stupid," hissed Karl. "He can't hear anything," and he reached out and grabbed Jimmy's arm, signing frantically at him. Two men in uniform appeared on the beach.

"Do something, get him to turn back," called Jess in a frightened voice.

"She's right," said Lindy grimly. "We can't risk getting taken in over there." Jimmy nodded at Karl and, revving up to a deafening roar he swung the boat round and raced away from the beach. Everyone fell back onto their seats and Lindy saw Jess reach out in terror to grab Sean. *Not such a great sailor then,* and she was about to speak when she felt the boat begin to buck slightly under their feet.

"What's the problem, are we running out of petrol?" she yelled to Karl over the engine noise.

Karl shook his head, "The tide is starting to turn." Jimmy was signing to him, pointing to his watch. "We haven't got much longer."

"Karl, tell him to go back to Hayling. My dad'll go ballistic," begged Jess.

"We can't turn back now," said Lindy, glaring at her.

"It'll be all right Jess, I promise," Karl said. "We'll just find that boat, grab what Lindy's cousin needs and we'll be out in a flash."

The sea was quite choppy now in the open water and Lindy was beginning to feel sick again. "Where now?" she said to Karl.

"Jimmy's heading for the old boatyard on the other side of Thorney Island. It's our only hope before the tide goes right out and leaves us stranded."

"Go for it."

The wind blew back Lindy's hair and made her eyes water. The sea was more choppy here and the boat bounced up and down. As she steadied herself against the rail, the sound of the engine reminded her of Karl's motorbike. *Will Karl buy another one? They must cost thousands.* Not for the first time she felt a deep pang of jealousy at the Lottery millions. *My mum and dad don't even pay the phone bill.*

"There!" cried Sean and, leaning forward, Lindy could see a large motor cruiser quite a long way from shore. It was moored to an orange buoy, chain clanking loudly as it rolled in the choppy water. *Trojan 3* was marked clearly on the side. Finally, they'd found it!

Jimmy slowed down and drew up alongside the boat. Lindy found it even harder to keep her balance as the deck swayed beneath her feet. She could see the rusty old boats on the shore in the distance which Garth had told her about. *Could Colin could be watching us right now? He might come after us, wouldn't take long to row out here. We'll have to be quick.*

"What a stupid place to keep a boat," said Jess, trying to comb her hair against the wind.

"I'm going up," said Karl, almost losing his footing as he climbed up the side of the little motorboat and grabbed for the deck rail above him. For a second his body swung free and Lindy was sure he would crash back down again. Then he was up and over.

She looked up to where Karl was leaning down, his arm outstretched. "Come on Lindy, you can do it."

"Yeah, all right, I'm coming," she called back, but secretly she was terrified of falling between the two boats. The water was so much deeper this far from the shore, deeper than anything she could imagine.

"Come on, we're running out of time."

Lindy swayed, her hands gripping the railing, feet sliding about on the moving deck. *I can't do it, I'll fall in and they'll never get me out this time.*

Panic rose inside her. The boat lurched and she fell heavily sideways, landing on her hip.

"You OK?" Karl called down.

Lindy lay there. The bright blue lettering of *Trojan 3* danced before her eyes. It seemed that the boat was mocking her, just like Colin and Elf had. "Shut your mouth, change the lightbulbs, take your money." Colin's voice bounced through her head in time to the rock and heave of the boats.

I've had enough; I've got to put a stop to it.

She hauled herself to her feet and cried out, "If you drop me, you're dead meat!"

Karl gave a short laugh and Lindy climbed up, reaching for the railing above her, hauling and levering herself as Karl grabbed her arms, until finally she landed on the deck of Colin's boat, panting triumphantly.

"Wait for me," Jess called out. She helped Sean to climb up and then she was up herself, throwing her arms round Karl's neck, making him lift her down onto the deck. She managed to lay her cheek on his and, catching Lindy's eye, she poked her tongue out.

In a fury Lindy grabbed the handle on the cabin door and shook it hard. *Jess thinks she can have anything she wants!*

"Wait," said Karl and he tried the door himself.

"Have you got the key?" said Jess, her hand still draped over Karl's shoulder.

Karl looked round at Lindy for support. She could see he had his knife, blade open, tucked in the palm of his hand. That's what he'd used to get into the houseboat. Musa's cousin had taught him how to do it.

"We don't need a key," chirped up Sean, "it's just a bit of a knack, Karl'll do it."

Lindy suppressed a smile and gave Sean a quick hug.

Karl wiggled the lock a couple of times and then the door sprang open. There was a steep ladder on the other side leading below. They trooped down, Lindy gripping the rope banister tightly as the boat threatened to throw her forward.

Everything in the cabin was very neat and clean. Just like Colin, nothing out of place, not a speck of dirt. Lindy thought back to that day in April when Colin had come to her house to offer her the job. *Must have made him feel really filthy sitting on our chairs and drinking out of our mugs.* How he must have hated that afternoon; he only put up with the family to get his claws into her. Colin had never come to the house before, had he? He used to meet Garth in the pub.

Looking round she could see that the walls were lined with comfortable-looking seats covered with bright cushions. There were drawers on one side and Karl immediately starting raking through them.

"What if he's taken it with him?" Karl asked.

Lindy was opening and shutting cupboard doors above the cabin seats. "It's got to be here," she said in a strained voice. Then, remembering Jess, she added, "After all, he *asked* us to get it." *This is the last chance, we've got to find it.*

"Come on, Karl, it's been a complete waste of time." Jess was trying to pull Karl back towards the steps. "We can't wait any longer to go back."

"I don't want to get stuck, Lindy," whined Sean, suddenly a little boy again, nagging at her.

"For God's sake!" Lindy banged in and out of a set of cupboard doors and then let out a whoop. "Here it is!" She felt weak with relief.

There was the sound of a horn beeping in constant staccato outside. "It's Jimmy," said Karl. "We have to go. The tide!"

Lindy tucked the laptop under her arm and they raced upstairs and back over the railings onto Jess's boat. They landed in a heap on deck as Jimmy revved to full throttle and turned the boat back, heading round Thorney Island towards Hayling again.

The boat bounced up and down more violently for a bit, and they all hung onto the railings. Lindy was sure she would be tossed into the sea. Sean was almost thrown over and she grabbed him and pulled him next to her, nearly dropping the laptop. The weather had changed since the morning. The sky was covered in dark clouds and the sea spread out like an icy grey sheet.

The coast of Hayling Island came into view and Jimmy signed rapidly to Karl. "We won't make it back to your boatyard, Jess," Karl said, looking anxious.

"We have to, Dad will go insane!"

"Jimmy says he can get down the channels while there's still water but we'll have to land somewhere nearer on Hayling before we get trapped in the mud. We don't have a choice." Jess sighed deeply and folded her arms.

They drove on and on and as Lindy stared towards the coast she could see the water receding from the mud flats. *If we get caught out here, it's all over. Colin will do his deals and me and Sean will have to run and hide and hope he never finds us.* She felt tears well up in her eyes but as she brushed them away Karl let out a shout.

"Look!" and following the line of his arm Lindy could see a jetty sticking out.

Deep water, just enough, please.

They all leaned over the side of the boat as Jimmy slowed the engine right down and eased the boat forward over the retreating tide. Lindy could see mud and pebbles, seemingly only centimetres beneath them.

"If he goes a-ground here we'll be stuck," said Jess.

"Don't be stupid," said Sean. "We can walk, it's not far."

"Too far in this mud. Once when I was little I walked away from my dad and started to sink. Dad had to heave like mad to get me out. He sunk to the top of his Wellington boots. Hayling mud sucks you in and never lets you go."

"In fact," said Karl in his I-love-facts voice, "several people a year do sink in the glutinous mud round Hayling. Up to their chests. They have to be rescued by helicopter."

"Wow!" said Sean. "A helicopter."

"Don't even think about it," glared Lindy. "Jimmy will get us in."

Sean gave a shrug.

"I told you so," said Jess with a smug grin.

As they approached the shore, the boat moving agonisingly slowly, Lindy was sure she could feel the hull scraping on the bottom. Sean leaned as far as he dared over the side, shouting up reports of how shallow the water was.

"Only about six centimetres left," he guessed wildly.

As they slid alongside the jetty, Karl jumped up, rope in hand, to secure the mooring. Lindy realised she was holding her breath and her heart was pumping hard enough to break a rib. But it was over; she was safe.

Chapter 31
Brains

Jess jumped off the boat, long hair flying, phone jammed to her ear. Lindy could hear snatches of an argument.

"No, just wait a minute… it wasn't like that Hector… no, we tried, but the tide… we did look at the time…" There was a long pause as Jess listened and then she said miserably, "Sorry. I'll make sure the boat is safe until we can get it tomorrow. Bye."

Feeling dizzy, Lindy leaned over the boat's railing and looked down at the mud. The harbour was almost completely clear of water now. The thought of getting stuck in that, up to her chest like Karl had said, made her shudder. *Would the crabs bite lumps out of my legs?* Something moved in the mud and she jumped back.

Climbing up onto the jetty felt worse than being on the boat. She could hardly stand upright, her legs swaying as though still at sea. The queasy feeling returned with a vengeance and, bending over, she suddenly threw up the contents of her stomach onto the squelching mud.

When she straightened Jess was smirking at her as usual. "We're back on dry land in case you hadn't noticed."

Lindy dragged her sleeve across her mouth, trying to wipe away the foul taste of vomit.

Karl touched Lindy's arm, "Are you OK?"

Jimmy produced a stick of gum from his pocket and Lindy took it gratefully. She watched as Jimmy signed to Karl.

"What's the problem?" she asked, unwrapping the gum.

"Jimmy's going to get his bike. He says he'd better go and face Hector too."

Jess gave out a dramatic moan. "My dad'll kill me, Hector's probably rung him by now."

They watched Jimmy set off towards some low buildings. They looked like holiday flats. No one had come out to see who they were yet.

But we haven't got long, we've got to find out what's on this stupid computer and when the deal is happening.

She held out the laptop to Karl. "Do you know how to work this thing?"

Karl took it cautiously, opened the lid and stared at the keyboard. Suddenly Jess leaned over his shoulder and pressed a button. The screen sprang into life and the start-up theme tune rang out.

"What's she doing?" snapped Lindy. She glared at Jess. "You can go home to Daddy now."

"Hang on," said Karl. He was scanning the screen hesitantly.

"I thought you were supposed to be a genius," said Jess with a mocking grin.

Karl shrugged. "Let's open the emails, see if what we're looking for is in there."

"Where did your cousin say the document was?" muttered Jess. She had taken the laptop from Karl and was sitting on the ground, moving the mouse around.

"Er, he didn't. He just needs to know where he's meeting someone tonight." Lindy hoped that would be enough and nothing on the computer would give too much away to Jess.

Jess typed 'Thursday' into the search box then clicked a couple of times.

"Is this it?" she said.

Karl leaned over and read out an email, "'Colin – meeting Thursday, 9.00 p.m., Room 537, tell E. Cheers. Dave.'" He glanced up at Lindy. "This must be it."

What was it Garth had said to her in prison? "Find out about all the business deals. You need details, sis. Dates, times, what they're dealing." His mate inside had said Elf and his South American dealers were bringing cocaine in by the tonne through the ports. "It's somewhere on that computer," Garth had said. "Find out, give it to the police and I promise, Colin and Elf will get twenty years."

Twenty years sounded so good. She'd be thirty-five by then, old and married with three kids. They'd never find her, would they?

"Look for Carlos," Garth had said. "That's the contact's name."

"Is there anything with the name Carlos?" Lindy asked.

"Why?" said Jess, shooting her a curious look.

"Just do it," Lindy snapped.

Jess shrugged and said in an irritated voice, "Can't see why you don't just take him the laptop and let him sort it out himself."

But Karl had his mobile in his hand, "No time now, he wants me to ring him once we get the details. What about looking in the spreadsheets, Excel?"

Jess moved the mouse around and clicked a couple of times. "Nothing there."

"Documents!" cried Lindy. "That's where I keep my stuff on the library computers."

"Don't you have one at home?" sneered Jess. "We've got four."

Lindy made a move towards Jess but she felt Karl's hand on her shoulder. Jess was staring at them, standing so close together and Lindy felt herself going red. She turned away and pulled her hair back more tightly in its band.

When she turned back Jess was focused intently on the screen, following the cursor, muttering, "Carlos, Carlos," to herself. Then she clicked the mouse and said, "This it?"

Karl took the laptop from her and read for a few minutes. A smile spread over his face and he said quietly, "Yes, that's it. Jess, you're a superstar."

Jess got to her feet, looking pleased with herself. Her phone rang and she frowned at the screen. "It's Dad. Now I've had it."

"Better answer it," advised Karl. He exchanged a look with Lindy.

I know exactly what you're thinking. We've got to get rid of her and Daddy will make her leave. It gave her a thrill to be able to read his eyebrows so clearly.

Jess pressed a key and put her phone to her ear. "Hi, Dad. No, it's fine... you don't need to... oh, Dad! That's so stupid... all right, all right... we're near Mengham, I think." She raised an eyebrow at Karl, who shrugged. Lindy had no idea where they were either and shook her head. "Sorry Dad... yeah, OK... see you."

Jess tucked her phone back in the pocket of her shorts and said, "He's on his way over. At least he can give us a lift into town." But her eyes were only on Karl.

"Your Dad's coming here?" said Lindy. They had to get out of there and quick. She looked round for Sean, who had wandered down to the water's edge. She ran after him, grabbed him and yanked him back up to the others.

"Karl?" Jess was saying.

Karl closed the laptop and stood up, his eyebrows set in an anxious line.

Say something you muppet, we can't let Jess's Dad find us, he might even bring the cops with him.

"I've got my physics homework, Jess, sorry," muttered Karl, his eyes on Lindy.

Jess folded her arms and stared from Lindy to Karl and back again. Then she pulled Lindy to one side and hissed in her ear, "You know what? Have him."

Lindy stared at her in astonishment. "What?"

"Come on," whispered Jess in her usual mocking voice. "You can see he's crazy about you, can't think why. He's all yours, too geeky for me anyway."

Lindy didn't know whether to feel relieved or just mad at Jess.

"Let's go," she called out to Sean and Karl.

Sean didn't take any notice and Lindy yelled at him, "Move, now!"

"What's the hurry?" called Jess as she watched them set off down the path.

"Sorry Jess," called out Karl over his shoulder, as they broke into a jog, "but thanks."

Then they were out of earshot and Karl led them off the road and into a small wood, saying, "We don't want to meet her dad on the way."

The wood was full of prickly bushes and Sean started to complain but Lindy pulled him along until they broke through onto the road.

Karl was still clutching the laptop. They sat down on a log and Lindy dabbed at a deep scratch on her leg. *That needs antiseptic.*

Karl broke into her thoughts, "Look at this email. *Tell E* must mean tell Elf, but what about Room 537? That could mean anything. It could be an office in any high-rise building!"

Lindy thought for a minute. "How about a hospital room? Elf's probably still in the hospital; they're having the meeting round his bed."

Karl shook his head. "The message was sent on Monday before the crash."

Sean was jiggling up and down, trying to get their attention.

"Do you need a wee?" asked Lindy.

"Dumbos!" yelled Sean.

"If you've got something to say," said Lindy, "say it or shut it."

Sean shrugged his shoulders and started to walk off, saying in a teasing voice, "Well, if you don't want to know…"

"This is insane," sighed Lindy. "Come on then, Brainbox, tell us what it means!"

Sean stopped, turned on his heel, cocked his head to one side and then said slowly, "What's got hundreds of rooms on Hayling Island?"

"The Lifeboat Station?" said Lindy.

"No!" Sean stood waiting, arms folded, toe tapping steadily on the ground.

Then Karl's face lit up. "You're a genius," he said, and Sean gave a broad grin.

"So, what is it?" yelled Lindy.

"The big hotel at the top of Hayling Island," said Karl. "It's got rooms on ten floors. They have business conferences there."

That was it, of course. It all fitted into place.

Lindy could suddenly picture the whole thing.

Colin would collect the holdall stuffed with all the little plastic packets of cocaine from the cannabis house.

Then he would drive to the hotel, looking like all the other businessmen in his suit, carrying the bag from hell. He would arrange to meet Elf, probably in the bar. They might have time for a quick drink, whisky and soda or vodka tonics. They would collect their key, go up to the room and wait for their buyers. More men in suits, with shed-loads of cash, would tap smartly on the door promptly at 9.00 p.m., and the deal would be done. Colin would be richer than ever and...

Lindy suddenly felt sick and dizzy. She leaned forward, put her head in her hands and closed her eyes. She could hear Karl murmuring to Sean, but there was a roaring in her ears and she couldn't make out the words. Then Sean was shaking her gently.

"Come on Lindy. We have to hitch a lift to Mengham."

"Why?"

"We need to use the Internet at the library," said Karl. "Email the documents to the police and then dump the computer. We stole it, didn't we?"

Like Elf's gun.

Chapter 32
Download

All Lindy could think about, as they stood up and scanned the road for cars, was time. Time cheating her like Colin and Elf. How soon before they were stranded and all this had been for nothing. It was already nearly five.

"Lot of traffic this time of the day," said Karl. "They'll stop for a little kid like you, Sean."

Sean took up a position by the kerb and stuck out his thumb. Three cars whizzed by.

"We need to get this info online or get a USB stick," Karl was saying, nodding at the laptop, "send the document to the police and then we need to get rid of it. It's got all our fingerprints on it."

"The lake where you threw the gun?" said Lindy.

Karl nodded.

Are we reading each other's minds now? Was Jess right about me and Karl or was it just that she couldn't be bothered to chase him any more?

A battered ex-army jeep driven by a windsurfer stopped and he let them sit in the back, on either side of an enormous board. As they bounced up and down through the Island, Lindy thought she was going to be sick again.

The surfer let them down near the library and they had

to walk past the secondary school. Lindy looked at the front gate longingly. *That's the school I should have gone to, far away from my brothers. I might have stood a chance there. That's where I want Sean to go, if we don't have to run away tonight. There's no way he's going to Park Road High like the rest of our family.*

The thought of maybe having to go on the run in the middle of the night made her feel so tired and miserable. Karl could disappear at any moment, couldn't he? What if his mum and dad suddenly called him like Jess's dad? *Would he go home, leave me and Sean to sort everything out by ourselves?*

But Karl's phone stayed silent and they finally reached the library.

"No!" yelled Karl and kicked the door. "It's shut on Thursdays! How're we going to get this stuff to the police now?"

"What are you lot doing here?" The voice was familiar.

Lindy spun round. It was Mr Davies, the English teacher. They stared at him, dumbfounded with shock.

"You weren't in English today, Lindy?" said Mr Davies, eyeing Karl and Sean up and down.

"The Social came round," said Lindy quickly, glaring at him. "What are you doing here?"

Mr Davies frowned at her rudeness but he said, "I came down to the Island for a meeting, not that it's any of your business. However, I'm glad we met." He paused, as if waiting for her to say something. Lindy tipped her head on one side and continued to glare rudely. Mr Davies gave a sigh and went on, "Seeing you has reminded me I need to speak to your parents about your progress. Or lack of it, I should say. Can't seem to get them on the phone."

"The phone's cut off," said Sean with a cheeky grin.

Mr Davies raised an eyebrow. "I see. Well, that's fine. I'll just have to go round and knock on the door, won't I?"

Lindy's heart sank. She couldn't have teachers snooping round the house. She was hiding so much.

Mr Davies was speaking again. "I might go over there now. I've got to drive through your estate to get home anyway. Won't be too late, will it?"

That means we can't go home now, he'll catch us out. But what if we need to grab our stuff and run off?

She realised there was nothing she could do and gave a shrug, "Whatever."

"Fine," said Mr Davies, pressing the remote on his car fob as he walked briskly away. A bright red Toyota winked from where it was parked outside the library.

"What now?" said Lindy when he'd gone.

"Newsagents," said Karl, pointing over to the parade of shops. They crossed quickly and Karl disappeared inside, coming out with a new USB stick. He tapped a message into his phone. The reply came quickly.

"Jimmy's on his way to pick us up," Karl said. "We'll download the document, then go back to the lake and get rid of the computer."

"And make sure Mr Davies doesn't spot us on his way off the Island to visit Mum and Dad," growled Lindy.

It was an anxious wait on the street for Jimmy but he finally appeared and pulled over. As they took off on the motorbike again, Lindy wished she was wearing a mask. It felt like the Island was full of spies, watching her every movement – Jess's Dad, Mr Davies, Bag Lady in the lane. Maybe she had already called the police about the funny smell from the cannabis house. Even Lindy had begun to smell it as she'd come up the path in the past couple of weeks.

Bag Lady's mad but she knows what's legal and what's illegal, doesn't she?

Once they got to the lake, Karl sat down on a bench, switched on the computer and downloaded the documents onto the USB stick. "Here you are Lindy. It's all yours."

Lindy took the stick and pushed it deep into the pocket of her jeans. This was the key to their escape; somehow she had to get it to the police without anyone knowing they were involved. *I'll do it on my own; Jimmy and Karl can take Sean away somewhere safe until this is all over.*

She watched as Karl took off his shoes, socks and jeans and waded into the lake until the water was above his knees. Then he hurled the laptop like a Frisbee. It skimmed through the air in a wide arc and landed in the reeds, sinking completely out of sight into the water.

"Job done," she said, as he reached the shore and started to dry himself with one of his socks. "I've got the USB stick as evidence, so I'll go to the police. You and Jimmy take Sean off somewhere, maybe to the funfair, eh Sean?"

Sean gave a cheer. "Wicked! We love rides, don't we Lindy?"

"Not me Sean, I've got some stuff to sort out. You stay with Jimmy and Karl, all the time, right?"

Karl stood up, tucking in his shirt, his eyebrows knitted in a deep furrow. "What do you mean, funfair? We're not going to any funfair!"

"This is the end, Karl," muttered Lindy. "You've done so much for me, but it ends here. Just go and forget about..."

"No way!" Karl shouted, his voice breaking. "Anyway you can't just walk into the police station. They'll take you in for questioning."

Lindy stared at her mobile.

"And you can't use that," Karl said. "They'll trace it."

"So what do I do?"

"Find a phone box."

"There's one up the road."

"No, it's too close to town, they'll send a squad car round as you're talking to them. And there are CCTV cameras all around here." Karl signed to Jimmy.

Jimmy thought for a minute and then signed back.

"There's a phone box Jimmy knows way out in the country near his mate's farm. He'll take us."

"But—"

"No buts Lindy. We have to keep moving, time's running out and we have to convince the police to raid that meeting. I'm still not sure how we're going to do that." Karl grabbed her arm and pulled her towards the bike.

"It's too dangerous, what about Sean and—"

Sean grabbed her other arm, "I'm safer with you Lindy, come on."

Then they were accelerating down the road, Sean snuggled on Lindy's lap in the sidecar, Karl clinging to Jimmy's broad back. As they crossed the bridge Lindy thought she saw Mr Davies' red Toyota ahead of them and she instinctively ducked down. The cannabis house and Bag Lady were behind them – but what lay ahead?

Jimmy took them along the motorway towards Chichester and then headed away from the main roads and into the countryside. They raced through village after village until they reached open farmland. Lindy couldn't see the time, her arm stuck between her and Sean, but it must be after six, maybe later. She could imagine Colin getting ready for his meeting. Would Elf be out of hospital and able to join him? Maybe he just had a bit of a bump on the head and he was OK now.

It took ages to get to the farm but finally Jimmy slowed the bike right down and pulled over into a lay-by. A phone box stood at the side. Lindy could see some farm buildings at the end of a long track between the fields. There was no one around.

"This should be safe enough," said Karl, climbing down from the bike.

As Lindy climbed out of the sidecar, Karl started to talk rapidly, "The main thing is to give nothing away about yourself, but to make sure they take you seriously.

Tell them where and when Colin is doing the deal, but nothing else. And do it quickly because they'll put a trace on the call immediately and send a squad car round to the phone box. That's if you don't want them to know it's you?" Karl stopped abruptly and looked at Lindy, his eyebrows arched in a quizzical curve.

"No way. If the police know, we'll all get into trouble. And Colin will find out. You know what he'll do – set his thugs on us. None of us will ever be safe again."

"I'm sure the police wouldn't put you in danger."

"You trust them that much?"

Karl thought for a moment and then shook his head. "You're right, it's too risky. In fact, the whole thing is too risky; I don't think you should phone them at all."

"What!"

Karl gazed into her eyes sadly, just the way he'd looked at her when he'd told her the story of Musa. "I'll phone them."

"No way, Karl. This is my mess, my scumbag family. I should never have—"

"Shut up, Lindy," said Karl in a voice Lindy had never heard before. He strode the last few yards to the phone box and opened the door, change jingling in his palm.

Lindy's shoulders dropped as she realised Karl was right. He could handle the police; it was the safest plan.

She squeezed into the box as he dialled. Karl put an arm round her waist and she nestled close and wished life could be this simple every day. Just a boy and a girl, phoning their friends, as they cuddled in a phone box. That's what ordinary teenagers with proper families did all the time, wasn't it?

Someone picked up at the other end and then Karl was giving the details in a terse voice.

"No names... guns... not yet, but they'll get away if you don't act tonight... It's all on the USB stick. I'll leave it in the phone box. No, I won't be doing any more. Just get them." He put the phone back on the hook and stared out the window. "Now we go home and wait."

"Are you kidding?" said Lindy.

Karl looked at her surprised.

"We go and watch. I need to see this, Karl."

"Me too," chirped up Sean.

Chapter 33
Mud Sucks

It was after seven and Lindy was beginning to panic that she would miss the action. *I've got to see Colin arrested, nothing else will do.*

She made one last effort to get rid of the others but Karl said, "We're in this together," and Jimmy gave a firm nod as Sean pushed her towards the sidecar.

The drive back to the Island seemed to take even longer than before. Jimmy took a couple of wrong turns before they reached the motorway. But finally they were riding over the bridge onto the Island and towards the hotel.

They needed to find somewhere to hide but it would have to be in full view of the building, otherwise what was the point? She couldn't wait to see the look on Colin's face when the police grabbed him. *He's going to hate their grubby hands all over him.*

When they arrived at the hotel, Jimmy drove into the car park and stopped the bike in a space in front of the main entrance. Two young men in wetsuits stood in the car park smoking. They looked at Jimmy's bike admiringly as Lindy hauled herself out of the sidecar. There was no sign of Colin and Lindy realised she had been steeling herself for a confrontation.

She looked around and pointed to a low wall at the end of the car park. "We could get behind that. No one will notice us there."

Karl nodded at the men in wetsuits. "Let's wait until they leave, so they don't see us hide."

I'll ram their ciggies down their throats if they don't finish soon. Lindy felt she could scream with the tension.

Finally, the men strolled through the hotel doors and Lindy led Jimmy, Karl and Sean quickly across the car park and over the wall.

It was a chilly evening with thick clouds obliterating the late sunlight. Lindy wished she'd brought a jacket. The tide had turned and was beginning to fill up the channels in the harbour, but there was still a wide stretch of mud and pebbles. Lights were coming on in the twilight on Langstone Bridge and along the eaves of the pub on the opposite shore. Lindy cast her eyes to the right where the old mill lay swathed in darkness. She wondered if anyone was messing about in the shallow lake behind the mill where Karl had thrown Elf's gun and the computer. What if someone found them and did tests and traced them back to Karl and Sean? No, there couldn't be anything incriminating now... could there? Wouldn't the water have washed away any evidence?

A weak moon was crowning through a small gap in the clouds, but it was almost dark and the lights of boats were appearing in the harbour, now filled with water again. The beach behind them was rapidly receding as the tide advanced. They waited and waited, but there was no sign of either Colin or the police and Lindy started to wonder if they had the wrong place. At ten-thirty, she whispered, "I'm going to take a closer look."

Karl looked at her nervously. "No, wait a bit longer Lindy, it's too dangerous."

Lindy stood up cautiously, peering over the wall. She couldn't just sit here, waiting and hoping, the time leaking away like the tide. *Colin has to get arrested and I have to make sure we're not spotted by the police, five minutes from the cannabis house and all that evidence.* Despite the cold she could feel sweat prickling in her armpits when she thought of her fingerprints on every surface. *And what about Karl and Sean? They've both been in the house too.*

A car swept past on the road, lights flashing over Lindy briefly and she heard the sound of music and laughter through the window. *Perhaps we got the wrong day, or maybe the police don't believe us and Colin and Elf will just do their business and disappear.*

"I'm going over to the hotel. I'll just check who's in Room 537," she said in a low voice. Before Karl could stop her, she ran across the car park and into the hotel lobby.

Then she heard footsteps behind her and, turning, she saw Sean run up, already wheezing and breathless. "You muppet," she hissed. "Get back to the others."

Sean shook his head, unable to speak, his hand clinging onto her arm. Something about his touch reminded her of Jemma, her little fingers holding tight when Lindy carried her upstairs.

Sean started to wheeze more loudly and Lindy shoved her hands into the pockets of his jeans, searching for the inhaler. Her fingers closed round it and she was pulling it out when bangs and shouts went out all round the lobby.

"Get down! Police! Out of the way!"

Two burly men with guns and bulletproof vests hurtled into the lobby. Lindy grabbed Sean and they made a dash for the exit, but as they tumbled out of the hotel they collided with a man running from the side of the building.

An iron hand gripped her wrist and a voice hissed in her ear, "Gotcha, you little cow. I should have known." She felt cold metal pressing against her cheek and she knew the voice instantly. It was Elf, his ears sticking out over a huge bandage wrapped around his forehead.

"Don't kill her!" Colin came up behind them. "She's our ticket out of here."

She felt Sean's thin little hand slide away, his panicky voice rising behind her. "Leave my sister alone, leave her alone!"

Then she was being pulled by Elf across the car park. She could still hear Sean calling her name and other, deeper shouts. The police?

"Where's the pick-up?" Elf shouted and he jerked the gun against her cheek.

Lindy let out a scream and Elf wrenched her wrist hard.

Colin yelled, "This way!" and they began to run down the road, half-dragging and half-carrying Lindy.

Lindy could hear more shouts from the police and sirens

starting up further away towards the bridge. They must be closing in. *They'll shoot Elf, he'll fall to the floor and his gun won't go off. It can't, it mustn't.*

But then Colin turned and bellowed, "Anyone comes near us, we'll blow her brains out!"

Lindy could hear feet pounding behind her and a voice called out, "Police! Stop! Drop your guns and let the girl go!"

"Don't shoot, she's my sister!" came Sean's voice from a long way off. Was he safe? And what about Karl and Jimmy? Lindy wanted to scream and scream but her jaw was frozen with fear.

Elf thundered on with Colin at his side, the gun pressed so hard into Lindy's cheek she could feel it jarring on her teeth. The police were all around them, sirens wailing, when Elf suddenly wrenched her to the left and threw her over a low wall. Her knees scraped on the bare brick. The pain was excruciating but Elf kept a vicious grip on her arm. Lindy thought she heard Karl cry out in alarm. But she didn't dare turn her head in case Elf fired the gun.

My cheek will explode to bits if he shoots! Her legs almost buckled with fear. *What if the police decide to fire anyway? They know who I am. Do they care if they hit me?* She could imagine what they were saying. *"She's only a Bellows, one less wouldn't matter. Take 'em down; we've got to get the drug dealers."*

"What we going to do, Col?" Elf was panting hard and shouting right in her ear.

"We've got to go along the beach." She saw Colin run past her and Elf pulled and pushed her along behind. She tried to scream again but all she could do was gasp as the gun pressed harder into her cheek.

"Keep running if you know what's good for you!" snarled Elf as he pushed her forward. But he was struggling to breathe.

How much longer can he keep going? He must still be woozy from the crash. She imagined him suddenly passing out; as he fell to the ground, she would grab the gun, swing round and fire repeatedly at Colin until he too dropped to the floor, his body twitching in its final death throes. The police would be astonished at her bravery and they'd give her a medal, telling her they'd never believed a Bellows could be so brave.

They had reached the pebbly beach and Lindy, taking advantage of Elf's flagging energy, cried out, "Let me go." It was very difficult to speak with the gun pressing into her cheek. She felt like she had a mouthful of metal.

Panting heavily Elf gasped, "Shut it," and, as if to drive the point home, jammed the gun harder into her jaw. Her teeth jangled and she squeezed her eyes shut, waiting for the blast from the barrel, choking with fear.

Colin turned and waved to the harbour. "The boat's out there, I can see one of the boys on it, they'll be waiting for the tide. Just a bit further, mate, and then we'll get away."

Elf stumbled a little and as Lindy looked up into his face,

she saw him close his eyes wearily for a second.

"Head's thumping like a drum," he muttered. "Not sure I can make it."

"Nearly there, mate, just hang on, we'll get this little cow into the boat and dump her later on."

Lindy struggled, trying to shake off Elf's grip.

Elf seemed too weary to respond but he didn't let go and then suddenly the beach ran out and they were running on mud. She could feel her feet squelching and water sloshed over her pumps. The tide was coming in rapidly. How much longer before they were right in the sea?

Jess's voice echoed in her tired mind. "We're studying the coastal features of Chichester Harbour." *Yeah, right, and most of that's mud.*

There's something worth remembering about the mud round Hayling Island. Something Jess told us as the boat raced the tide back to shore. But Lindy couldn't think straight with the gun pushing into her cheek and her exhausted legs threatening to give way. The water was getting deeper and it was cold enough to make her shiver. Up ahead she could see Colin was almost up to his waist.

"Nearly there, mate," he yelled over the sirens screaming across the bridge. Lindy felt her ears would burst with the noise and the fear.

How much longer before Elf pulls the trigger and kills me? Will I see Jemma again when I'm dead?

Lindy saw the outline of a small motorboat on the water ahead and what looked like a torch flashing. All part of Colin's plan. *I'll bet there's more drug dealers in that boat. They'll never let me go. Elf will shoot me out at sea and Sean will never find my body. I want to be buried next to Jemma!*

She would have wailed it out loud if the gun wasn't pressed so hard to her cheek.

Then she heard a desperate cry from Elf. "My feet, Col! I'm stuck."

Colin turned, his arms splashing in the sea. "Pull, mate. Come on, we're almost at the boat."

Then Lindy remembered what Jess had said. "The mud round Hayling Island sucks you in, never lets you go."

Lindy felt the loosening of Elf's grip on her arm and the gun slid from her cheek. *This is my chance,* she thought, and, suddenly alert, she lunged backwards, wrenching her feet with the last of her strength. As Elf dropped the gun into the water, she stumbled to one side and staggered backwards.

Karl called it glutinous mud. "Glutinous means sticky like glue," he had told her in his I-love-facts voice. Hayling mud will suck the boots from your feet and nothing will get you out, except the coastguard with his helicopter, pulling you up with all the strength of its massive rotor blades.

But now the mud had come to her rescue. Not Liam or Garth or anyone else in her rubbish family. Not even Karl. It was the beautiful, glorious mud of Hayling Island, trapping the criminals and their stinking guns in its glutinous grip.

At each movement, Colin and Elf sank further and

further down. Colin, the shorter of the two, was already up to his chest in water. She could see his eyes, wild with fear. Elf, exhausted, gradually stopped struggling and looked like he was about to keel over.

Colin screamed at her, "You little cow, wait till I get you."

"I don't think so!" yelled Lindy. She could feel rock beneath her feet and knew she wouldn't sink any further.

Just have to wait to be rescued, they can't touch me now.

Suddenly, there was a heavy boom in the distance. Looking round Lindy saw a bright orange light blossoming in the distance to the right of the hotel. Fire! And it was coming from the direction of the lane where the cannabis house was. She stood and stared for a minute and then it slowly dawned on her. The house was on fire. All those fingerprints, stray strands of hair and pieces of skin, full of hers and Karl's and Sean's DNA, were going up in smoke.

Garth had said he would get one of his mates to torch the house, but she didn't really think it would happen.

"Take a look, Col," she yelled, pointing behind him. "Know what that is? Your filthy, illegal cannabis farm on fire. The whole lot is going to burn to the ground." She let out a whoop of joy and pumped her fist in the air.

Colin twisted round to see, and then turned back to her, his eyes shining with fury. "I thought I could trust you." His voice dropped to a wheedling whine. "Come on Linds, we're family, remember?"

"You should know, cuz!" Lindy yelled back joyfully. "Can't trust a Bellows."

The flames lit up the whole sky behind the hotel. There wouldn't be a trace left. The police would never know she had been there.

Chapter 34
Legal

"Glutinous."

"What's that, son?" Mum was spooning a great dollop of porridge into Sean's bowl.

"It means sticky like glue, don't it Lindy?" Sean squirted chocolate sauce all over his porridge and stirred it in. The spoon almost stood up in the dense, grainy mass.

Glutinous had become their favourite word. In the days after the police raid, when Lindy was too scared to go outside in case one of Elf's mates shot her dead, she sat in the living room watching TV. Dad let Sean have the remote and everything they watched was classified as 'glutinous', like Japanese rice on the cooking programmes, or 'not glutinous', like ice-cream.

One night, Sean insisted on watching open-heart surgery and, as blood pumped into the gaping chest cavity, he yelled out, "Blood! That's glutinous."

"No, it's not," said Lindy, thinking of how the blood ran when she cut herself. Then she remembered its stickiness on her hand and a line from *Hamlet*, 'Now I could drink hot blood. And do such bitter business as the day would quake to look on.'

It had all been such a bitter business and now that it was

over, Lindy still couldn't believe she was safe.

That awful night, after they'd been pulled out of the mud and Colin had yelled, "I'll kill you!" before the police had dragged him away, she had just wanted to curl up under her duvet with TerryTed and never get up again.

But she wasn't allowed, was she? The house filled up with police and social workers and other people who didn't say what they were there for. Everyone wanted answers to a million questions and Sean kept saying stupid things like, "We didn't know he was growing cannabis."

Yeah right, as if a Bellows wouldn't know what Colin was up to. She could see the scorn in their eyes.

Lindy didn't speak. She had decided to become a mute like Karl. She missed Karl's silence, riding around on the back of the bike, his sweet salty smell as she clung to him. Were the police questioning him too?

If we never speak again then no one will ever know what we did.

The social worker's name was Wendy. She wore a tight little jacket and black trousers. Lindy was wondering what kind of family she had when Wendy started saying to Mum, "We could consider Sean going into respite care for a few weeks with a foster family—"

"Never!" shrieked Mum, so loud that Lindy thought the lightbulbs would shatter.

Everyone stopped talking and the room went very quiet, except for one big sob which Mum let out. Dad put down the TV remote and put his arm around her. Sean crept across the floor and pushed himself into the tiny space between the telly and the wall, his dirty thumb stuck in his mouth. Lindy hadn't seen him suck his thumb for years.

"I said Colin were proper no good, eh Colleen?" muttered Dad.

"Sure enough you did and we didn't listen," said Mum in a creaky little voice. "And what with the big ones away and the baby..."

She stopped and the social worker looked down, shuffling her papers.

"I couldn't lose another one. And we can manage. Can't we, Lindy?"

For the first time in her life, Lindy's family were looking at her as if... as if they really needed her. Sean looked so tiny and helpless in his corner, like Jemma used to look after her bath. That woman could whisk him away in her shiny Vauxhall Astra any minute now and Mum would go to pieces.

If Garth were here he would know what to do.

But he isn't, Lindy, whispered a little voice in her ear. *It's down to you.*

It was then she realised she couldn't be like Karl and tuck herself away, refusing to speak. She had responsibilities, didn't she?

"What's the problem?" she said, glaring at the social worker. "I can take Sean to school, can't I Mum?" Lindy threw her mum a look and she nodded back. "You can do the housework like always, I'll help. And anyway, whatever, the family stays together. Right, Sean?"

It's about time, isn't it?

Sean nodded, making big sucking noises on his thumb, his eyes wide and fixed on Lindy.

Wendy gave a cautious nod. "That would be very helpful Lindy, just until your mum gets back on her feet."

"I always managed with Lindy's help now, didn't I girl?"

After that Lindy sat in silence as the Social and the police went on and on about food and school uniforms and cleaning the house up and other dumb stuff.

"You'll have to bring Lindy to the police station on Monday morning, Mr Bellows," said a huge policeman.

Lindy stiffened. *What if they make me speak to Colin?*

"What for?" said Dad suspiciously. "She ain't done nothing wrong. It was all that nutter, Colin. He's the one you oughta be talking to."

"Sure enough, it is terrible hard what he's gone and done to this family. Destroyed us, he has, destroyed us."

Mum looked close to tears again and Lindy reached out and took her hand. It was skin and bone. Her mother clutched her as if she was clinging to a lifeboat out at sea.

I thought Colin had come to rescue me after Jemma. How wrong can you be? Now I have to do the rescuing. Lindy wondered what Joyce would say if she could see her now, comforting her mother with a proper bedside manner.

"Drugs are a serious business," said the policeman in a stern voice.

Lindy felt herself go cold. Here it was, the nightmare she

had been waiting for all these weeks. Prison.

But then Wendy went over and muttered to the policeman. He looked at Lindy as if weighing her up and then he said a bit more gently, "I shouldn't worry too much, what with Lindy being under the influence of her older cousin, it'll probably be a reprimand. But we do need some questions answered."

"So I'm not going to prison?" Lindy blurted out, going red as everyone turned to look at her.

"Good heavens, no!" said Wendy. "That was never a possibility. We'll get you some help in the house, Mrs Bellows, just till things settle down. You've all had such a hard time since the baby died, haven't you?"

Mum let out a huge sigh and for a minute Lindy felt as if all the air was sucked out of the room.

Every sad thought...

She wished Garth was here to make a joke, put a smile back on Mum's face. Mum caught her eye and they exchanged a look. *She wants me to say something, to speak for the family. What is there left to say?*

The truth.

"We loved baby Jemma and we miss her very much, don't we Mum?"

"We do that, Lindy, girl. Miss her something terrible."

Over the following days, as Mum started to get dressed in the morning and make porridge for breakfast, Lindy wondered if she would ever see Karl again. She tried phoning him but his mobile seemed to be disconnected. She wanted to tell him she'd been reprimanded by the police and it would stay on her record for years, but at least it wasn't prison.

When they got home from the police station, Wendy was there. Mum borrowed her phone to call the prison; she'd arranged a phone call with Garth. When it was Lindy's turn she took the mobile into the kitchen.

Garth was triumphant. "You did good, sis. You won't see Colin and Elf again."

"But what about their mates? You said they'd come after me," said Lindy. "I'm too scared to go outside on my own. I keep thinking someone's going to shoot me."

"You don't need to worry. My mate says they caught all of them, the whole smuggling ring. There's no one left to bother about a little kid like you."

It was as though a huge block of concrete had lifted from Lindy's shoulders. She was safe. It was the first time in months she'd felt like that. She spent a lot of time out in the street on her pink-and-white Heeleys, with Sean scooting around beside her on Garth's old skateboard. The wounds on her arm had begun to fade and she could wear short sleeves in the warm July sunshine.

After a few days, Wendy took her to buy a new uniform. "It's not worth it," Lindy grumbled. "There's less than two weeks left of term."

But actually she was looking forward to going back to school. Wendy let her buy a skirt which was quite short with a zip down the back, like Jess wore. It was the first time in years she'd had any new uniform.

It was a hot July Monday when she walked back through the school gates with Dad and Wendy. They met the Head who seemed embarrassed to see her.

"I've spoken to the teachers, Lindy, and everyone is going to make sure you get extra help to catch up. Mr Davies seems to think you could do very well in English."

He knows he shouldn't have let me go with Colin that day. He's probably in big trouble.

But she couldn't see the point of making a fuss. She might as well go back to lessons and get on with it.

It was English first thing. Lindy scanned the classroom as she went in; no sign of Jess. That was a bit disappointing. She wanted to show off her new skirt.

"Sit down Lindy, page 126," said Mr Davies and he handed her an open book. "We're at the end of the play but I'll help you catch up."

A snigger went round the class but Mr Davies silenced them with a glare and said, "Read on, Alix."

Alix caught Lindy's eye and nodded to something in her hand. It was a note. Lindy took it as she went past to her seat. She read it when the teacher wasn't looking.

Want to sit with me and Kim at lunch? We heard what happened. Jess is ill in hospital but Karl's back today.

Her heart gave a little jump. Karl was back. I'll go and find him the minute the bell goes.

Alix was reading aloud in a clear voice and Lindy was caught by Horatio's words as Hamlet is stabbed,

"'Now cracks a noble heart. Good night sweet prince, And flights of angels sing thee to thy rest.'"

Then Alix read the stage direction, "'Hamlet gives a long sigh and dies.'"

Lindy let out a gasp and, without thinking, said, "Hamlet's dead? I wasn't expecting that."

Mutters of agreement went up round the room. There were a couple of titters about brainless Bellows too, but Lindy ignored them. Her mind felt as though it was scrambling to make sense of it all.

Sweet prince. That's another sad thought to add to the list, isn't it?

So Hamlet never found a safe refuge on earth.

That could have been me caught in Colin's vile trap.

She thought of Garth singing 'Danny Boy' and how the girl imagined herself dying, almost as if there is something good or heroic about dying. But Lindy knew better, didn't she? Jemma's death had been such a waste.

That's not going to happen to me. Colin and Elf thought they owned me. They thought they decided if I lived or died. But they were wrong! I own me, I decide!

At the end of the lesson Lindy stopped at Alix's desk. "See you in the lunch hall in five?"

Alix nodded and said, "Great."

Even Kim gave her a bit of a smile, so that was OK.

Then Lindy took off down the corridor, determined to find Karl amongst the noisy, pushing crowd.

Suddenly she felt a familiar touch on her shoulder.

"Thought you'd disappeared," said Karl as she turned around.

"Not that easy to get rid of a Bellows."

They fell into step and went out into the playground, Karl pulling open the heavy door for her.

"Tried to ring you," said Lindy.

"Dad cancelled the contract. And the credit card," said Karl, squinting in the bright sunshine.

They looked at each other in silence for a bit and then Karl said, "What are you doing in the summer?"

"Got a job. Joyce, my trainer in the Ambulance, she has a kennels." Lindy pulled a lollipop out of her pocket and began to peel off the wrapper. "What about you?"

"Mum and Dad have gone to Batan."

"You what?"

"It's an island off Singapore."

Lindy shrugged. A football rolled towards them and Karl kicked it back to a group of boys.

"Are you sleeping in the houseboat?" asked Lindy, rolling her tongue around the sticky lolly.

Karl shook his head."I'm staying at Jimmy's. Helping out at the boatyard over the summer. Then I'm going back to Portsmouth Grammar School, and I'll be living with Jimmy's aunt and uncle. The Mackintoshes." He said the name with obvious relish. "They're really nice. Got a whole room full of books."

"Oh well, that's all right then."

Karl threw her a nervous look as if scared she would

start insulting him again.

She could hear all those words she'd spat out at him when they first met: *muppet, retard, thicko*. She felt her stomach churn at the memory.

"How about you?" said Karl.

"They're giving me extra lessons to catch up. That's what they do with sad cases."

"You're not a sad case, Lindy."

"I got a reprimand by the police."

"But not prison."

They walked on for a bit in silence and then Karl said, "What about Sean?"

"The Social have put him in summer camp for the holidays to keep him out of trouble. They don't want another Bellows boy in prison." She paused, and then she said, looking into the distance, "At the kennels I'll have my own puppy. Going to call her Jemma."

They fixed each other with an unblinking stare.

Then Karl leaned forward and kissed her on the lips for such a long time they both ran out of air.

He gently pulled away, his eyebrows settled in a long black line. "Thanks, Lindy."

"What for?"

"For rescuing me."

"You make me sound like Spiderman."

"Terminator, more likely," and they both burst into helpless, silent laughter.

Note from the Author

I was a teacher for many years in London schools and worked with young people who had special needs. Many of my pupils had communication problems and some of them were mute, like Karl in this novel. Children stop speaking for all sorts of reasons and once they stop it is very difficult for them to start again. Many children and teenagers who are mute do speak perhaps to one friend, or they speak at home. But school can be a very difficult place for them. In Karl's case he stopped speaking altogether. He might not have started again for years if he hadn't found a friend he could trust in Lindy. Many children who are mute benefit from special professional help to gain the confidence to speak again.

I have worked with teenagers who have severe emotional and behavioural problems and sometimes self-harm. One girl was so scared of the world she grew a spearnail, like Lindy, for protection. But, like Lindy, she was able to turn her life around.

Some of the young people I knew became schizophrenic after taking cannabis. This inspired me to research and write about the link between mental health problems and drug abuse. If Lindy's story helps even one teenager think twice about taking drugs, then it's been a story worth telling.

About Miriam Halahmy

Miriam Halahmy has published novels, short stories and poetry for adults and young people. Her stories and poems have been included in anthologies, read on the radio and performed on stage. Her novels are constructed around strong characters and real-life situations. Miriam believes that all young people have a future, and that fiction can offer a route map forward.

A Londoner all her life, Miriam's family lived on Hayling Island for twenty-five years and she has been visiting the Island regularly since the 1970s. She decided to set her novels there because of its beauty and mystery. Her favourite time on Hayling is the winter, when the Island is at its most peaceful.

Miriam continues to write and publish poetry, articles and book reviews. She has completed her cycle of three novels set on Hayling Island and is planning future novels for young adults. In her spare time she regularly escapes her London home to walk on the Hayling beaches, and hunt for shells and fossils along the shoreline.

www.miriamhalahmy.com

Acknowledgements

Many thanks to those trustworthy and supportive fellow writers who commented on drafts of this novel, especially Loulou Brown, freelance editor and writer, who provided such wise insight.

A particular thanks to the sailors and coastguards around Chichester Harbour who patiently listened to my constant questions and advised me on the tides and sailing aspects of this novel. Any errors in the narrative are entirely my own.

For always making me feel so welcome, a big thanks to the Hayling Islanders, many of whom have commented enthusiastically on my first Hayling novel, *Hidden*. I hope you will find *Illegal* just as intriguing a portrait of your beautiful Island home.

Thanks to my agent, Eve White, who ensured the complete cycle of novels found a publisher. And many thanks to everyone at Meadowside Children's Books, especially Lucy Cuthew, my editor.

Every word in this novel has been carefully read by my husband, Rafael, who remains my constant in a world as unpredictable as the sea.